"Full-bodie[...] friendship, desire, and asp[...] captures a young man's contradictory attitudes: what he wants, what he believes he knows, and how he senses he's crossing a threshold into the rest of his life. At seventeen, eighteen, one could fall in love, fall into the bottle, even fall out of life. Cebulski weaves a frank and tender gay story."

Tucker Lieberman, author of *Bad Fire*

"It Helps with the Blues is a raw look into the tumultuous world of teenage love and loss. This coming of age story is a tour de force of emotions and self-discovery. Navigating what it means to find oneself while losing others along the way, the young narrator takes readers on a complicated journey of introspection they won't soon forget. With almost reckless abandon, he wanders through the threads of this story teetering on the edge of his own inborn privilege and a need to turn his back on it all in favor of his own 'humble inadequacy'. This story burns through and through, and stays with you long after its simmering outcome."

Kevin Craig, author of *The Camino Club*

A tRaum Book
Munich, 2022

Cover art by Oliver Grin

tRaum
Books

It Helps with the Blues

by Bryan Cebulski

Table of Contents

1 – Ice at the bottom of the glass

We clinked glasses, leaned back in lawn chairs on the bar roof and admired the sky through light-polluted air.

A breeze brushed past, a sign that the always cruelly short Midwestern fall was shifting to winter. Still, the coolness seemed to soften Jules, put her into a state of mind that made talking with her less intimidating. I managed to go almost half an hour without pissing her off.

"You're never going to college?" she asked.

"Probably not," I said, sipping the last of a whiskey sour, the smell of freshly squeezed lemon and lime still on my fingers, then setting it aside. "For now at least. I've resigned myself to a life of humble inadequacy."

"Humble inadequacy? Oh my god, fuck off."

She was easily bored, I found, and so always at least half confrontational in her conversations with me. Always digging, trying almost unintentionally to get people to remove their defenses and get to the more complicated layers of their beliefs and lives.

"I mean, think about it from my point of view," I argued, an ill-advised attempt to defend myself, though a maneuver she absolutely wanted me to take. "I don't wanna take for granted that I've been born with a small empire to inherit. I'll work here or at another one of our places awhile and eventually, probably, take them over."

"So you're going to be a dumbass, a bougie leech, and an alcoholic."

"More or less. Hey, I can still study in my free time."

"Whatever. What's your dad got to say about this?"

"For the time being, I'm saying I'm taking a gap year. He won't care though."

"Like hell he won't. You're supposed to go to some bullshit liberal arts university on a legacy scholarship and major in business and economics."

"You know, you're the last person I thought'd be lecturing me about college."

That got her. Jules scooted upright, tucked her knees in, and lay her cheek against them.

She turned her head and looked at me—really looked at me—and said, "I expect a lot from you is all. To get out of this town, meet new people, make an impact…"

"Yeaaah," I conceded. "But this is a good fit for me. I'm not like you. You're going to be the next Joan of Arc and make a ridiculous impact."

She cracked up at that.

"Me, Joan of Arc?"

"Why not?"

"I'll be lucky if I end up the next Amy Winehouse."

"That seems disrespectful to Miss Winehouse."

"Fair enough. What I mean is, I'll be lucky if I do anything even remotely noteworthy and then get horribly maligned and spiral out in my late twenties." She took a sip of her own whiskey sour, ice clanking against glass. "Look, the big secret is I only wanna sit around and get high all day. I need to do something meaningful just so it's justified."

"You know you don't mean that."

She shrugged.

"Well, half serious."

Bryan Cebulski

I had set up a Bluetooth speaker on a card table and put Bill Evans' *Conversations with Myself* on repeat. Jules had asked me to recommend her classy music. "So I can sound sophisticated at the cocktail parties I'll be attending in my 20s." She went to me for things like that—books, movies, cool jazz, fancy drinks.

Jules swished her glass around again and watched the ice cubes shift.

"This is good, by the way," she said.

She had the ability to make small warm remarks like that linger. I appreciated it, even though there was no mixology technique worth complimenting.

We had a weak crowd at the bar tonight, as expected. If you paid attention long enough, you could feel out the rhythm of Hyde's Place's nightly popularity. There was at least one quiet weekend every month. This was one of them. I don't know, people must work extra shifts or spend more time with their loved ones or catch up on lost sleep. Hyde's Place appealed to people like that—traditional but amicable middle-class men and women looking for a peaceful retreat after work. The bar developed such a reputation over the years. It was my favorite of my family's establishments.

"Well, anyway, thanks for getting me drunk," Jules said.

She did this sometimes, abruptly changed the subject. Put our argument into her back pocket, where it would remain until she was sufficiently pissed off at me again.

"No problem," I said. "Still can't believe you love whiskey."

"I like a lot of things I'm not supposed to."

"Like?"

"Mm... well, I guess hard liquor and weed mainly. Douchey leftist punk stuff. Another big secret is I'm the textbook case of punk teen girl-dom."

"That does fit."

"And you're the textbook case of overprivileged white male who's too lazy to go to college."

"All those?" I asked. Apparently it didn't take her that long to get sufficiently pissed off again.

"Yup."

"I wouldn't call me lazy," I tried to reason. "Unambitious at worst. What was wrong with 'humble inadequacy'?"

"Oh my god, fuck off," Jules said, laughing. She took another sip. Her dark auburn hair rustled slightly in the wind. Otherwise her body was static, photographic.

Then she added, lowering her voice, lips barely moving, "I guess you do have it made here."

I lowered my head, circled my finger around the rim of my empty glass.

"Can't complain."

We sat there. I wondered what Jules thought of Bill Evans, but she wasn't really listening. Not surprising. Jules was always somewhere else. Neither up in the clouds nor in her own little world, but in some dreamy foreign idyll unknown to the rest of humanity. She stared at the sky, the glow of suburban lights. She seemed stuck on something, some thought or feeling.

A little later, I went downstairs to make us another round. I decided to drink plain sweet vermouth this time, which I knew would horrify Jules, but the taste of it called to me. I made another whiskey sour for her, this time with bourbon. I figured she wouldn't notice; she didn't pay much attention to taste. Not that she was unrefined or simple or anything—it was just something she didn't feel the need to focus on.

Back on the roof, Jules had her phone in her hand. Her eyes were fixed on the screen, her face lit with blue. She was scanning a text message. She looked at me, then back at the phone.

"Uhh... shit."

"What's up?"

"It's this friend... I hate to ask, but you think he could maybe join us?" She asked this in a particular way, innocently aware that it was impossible to refuse. At least that's how it seemed to me. "I'm really worried about him. He's sending me these really long texts about all the majorly depressing shit that's been going on with him. He should prooobably be around people."

I tried to hold back my disappointment.

"No, no, that's cool," I said, hoping to sound sincere. "Who's the friend?"

"Dennis Tucker. Know him?"

"Dennis Tucker... Dennis Tucker, the sophomore?"

"That's the one."

"Yeah, his gym locker's like right next to mine."

Quiet, inward guy, I thought. Probably gay or queer in some way, though not out. There were only rumors and how he acted to give that impression.

"How do you know him?" I asked.

"He used to be my little brother's friend, and I used to hang out with his big sister before I got sick of her. Always kind of got along better with him than her, actually. We usually just text or talk online though. He's a sweet

11

kid. Let's cheer him up and get him drunk."

"In that order?"

"Whatever order works. Thanks for this, honestly. I owe you."

Jules typed out a text, then put her phone back in her pocket. She snatched her refilled glass and gulped half of it down.

Dennis called her fifteen minutes later.

Jules, phone to her ear, told me he was in the parking lot across the street. I told her to tell him to cross the street and go around back and we'd let him in. She relayed the message. After a few "uh-huh"s and an "okay hun," she hung up.

"Well, he's definitely been crying or something."

"Uh-oh. What drink helps best with broken hearts?"

"You should know that," she said flatly. "C'mon, he's waiting."

We went downstairs by a narrow staircase in the back. I opened the employee-only exit.

There, standing in front of the dumpsters, was a tiny silhouette.

"Hey," I said, waving him over. "Come in."

He stepped forward a couple paces. For a few seconds, I saw him in the light, caught a glimpse of red teary eyes under a mop of dirty blond hair, before he rushed to Jules. He buried his head against her collarbone, sniffling and quivering like a sick puppy.

Jules rubbed his back.

"There, there. Mama's gotcha," she said it with zero irony.

I went to the bar to get a bottle of something new while they went to the roof.

Gordon was there, talking to an old man across the counter. Our bartender was a trusted family friend, and for all intents and purposes, an uncle, who had been working at Hyde's Place for at least two decades now. He had a limitless supply of energy, singlehandedly infusing life into any room he walked into.

This was one of many times I'd brought a friend over. Not that he minded. He'd been a teenager in San Francisco in the 70s and had a fiendish idea of what normal teen activity was. Alcohol was child's play. He probably would have let us snort amphetamines if we'd wanted. He probably would have gotten them for us himself.

"What's up, kid?" he asked.

"I need a bottle of something," I said, my eyes scanning the liquor.

"Something? Never heard of that brand!"

Either he purposely made jokes like this to make me cringe or actually had the corniest sense of humor. I could never tell.

"What's the best brand for a broken heart?"

"You should know that. What else but cheap vodka?"

He took a bottle from the top shelf and gave it to me. It looked like it'd been up there for some time. Wasn't even labeled.

"Get rid of this for me, will ya?" he said. "It's the worst of the worst. Might as well have just stuck a rotten potato in a bottle."

I unscrewed the cap and took a whiff. Definitely vodka.

"Uh, sure. Thanks, Gordon," I said.

"I'll just put that on your tab. You still owe me for

all that cocaine." He said this loudly and with a smile, amusing the half-dozen patrons, turning their attention away from the TV for a moment.

"Oh I'll pay you back soon."

"You better! That was quality coke!"

He went back to talking to the old man. I saw some of the patrons looking at me. They probably knew I was underage, but met my presence with a shrug. As long as my inhibitions weren't shot to the point of blacking out or alcohol poisoning (and I made sure to never reach that point), I was perfectly welcome.

My father's rules for me in and around the bars were pretty relaxed in general. He seemed to have stopped caring once he realized that his inherited wealth and local influence gave him the ability to make anything involving the phrase "underage worker labor infractions" disappear. And besides, by the time I'd turned seventeen, he felt I was more than mature enough to spend some quality time within the establishments that comprised his life's—our whole family's—work.

Plus, ever since the divorce, he'd wanted to establish himself as the "fun" parent. He could be trusting of me to a fault. It's just his luck that I'm a more or less reserved person.

I grabbed three glasses, filled an ice bucket, and took a bottle of the fancy cranberry juice from the fridge. Arms satisfactorily full, I went back up to the roof.

Bill Evans played "Stella by Starlight." The music emanated so low that my memory of the song filled in for the keystrokes.

Above the piano, a young man sobbed.

Dennis was curled up in Jules' arms. He made feeble attempts to stop, but couldn't hold out for long before a loud heaving whimper came on and he exploded into another bout of wails. Jules' sleeve was soaked and stained with tears and snot. Semi-drunk as I was, I still noticed the extraordinary way Jules nurtured the poor guy. Her eyes were closed, her face solemn as the Virgin Mary, and a soft "*Shh, shh…*" escaped her lips as she rocked the boy back and forth. I almost felt jealous.

I tended to the drinks. I set everything down on the card table, dropped a few ice cubes into each glass, and poured equal amounts of vodka and cranberry juice.

Dennis looked up as soon as the drinks were poured. He withdrew from Jules, jumped to his feet, scampered over to the table, and not skipping a beat, just slammed them all down. One-two-three.

I stared at him. No idea why I didn't intervene. One of those train wreck situations.

Then he took the bottle of vodka and started chugging it. His Adam's apple bobbed up and down. It must have been burning holes in his throat. He downed four swigs before his cheeks puffed with the contents of his stomach and he slammed the bottle back down and ran to the edge of the roof. He was lucky to get there in time. I heard noises like a boar drowning in mucus.

Jules resumed her nursing. I went downstairs for some water. Maybe for some booze free of pukey backwash too.

Dennis Tucker. Dennis Tucker, the sophomore who shared my PE hour, who I'd never spoken to aside from pleasantries, and even then only bare-bones pleasantries. My knowledge of the kid was limited to a general idea of his character: shy, frail, cute. Not my type: Too young

15

and not self-realized enough, so I never even thought to engage with him in that way. He probably had at least a few friends, but I never saw him with anybody.

I wondered if this all had something to do with a bad coming out scenario. Felt like that was usually how it went. I wanted to ask him whether this was the case, but even in my semi-addled state, I couldn't bring myself to just blurt it out. He might get offended, which would have only made things worse. And, most important for me, it risked me getting on Jules' bad side.

So I said nothing. Poured water for him. He slowly sipped, eyes downcast. He turned up the music, pressing the plus button on the speaker over and over, probably to drown out his own thoughts. Curiously, after he heard it once, he kept going to my phone to put "Spartacus Love Theme" back on over and over.

Jules rubbed his back or ran fingers through his too-long hair, smiled at him, let him know somebody cared. She drank water too, hoping to sober up before the night was over.

I drank my cranberry juice and vodka with vodka out of the new bottle, feeling slightly bitter. A lot of me resented Dennis for ruining my night with Jules. I tried to feel bad for him, tried to summon some sympathy. I wished I could have been as caring and patient as Jules, but thinking about it just made me angry. The poor little boy became just too pathetic. His quivering lips, his unwillingness to talk, the tears. It was so maddening to look at, to hear, to be a part of.

I thought about what a tougher guy than me might say, what he would say to Dennis. "You think you're the only person in this world who's in pain? You think you're so special you deserve pity? Fuck your pain. Fuck pity. Fuck being special. The world has no need for wimps. The world has no need for more self-loathing assholes. At the very least, confide with these people. Tell them about your little issues. Let them in. They're here to help and you're just being a whiny punk." I thought these things. I said nothing.

An hour went by somehow. Not a peep from Dennis. The night ended with an awkward parting of ways. Jules drove him home. I stayed on the rooftop and watched them go. Did they even tell me they were leaving? My senses were so numb that I couldn't remember the next morning. My mind regressed with each silent minute, until the whole outside world collapsed in on itself.

My phone died, killing off the sounds of Bill Evans along with it. I took the speaker and folded up the card table and chairs and went downstairs. Hyde's Place was long closed, the employees gone. The frustration I'd felt earlier in the night was replaced by pitiful melancholy.

With defeat exacerbated by drink and with nothing else to do, I passed out in one of the booths.

I keep dwelling on this night.

Gradually, more and more over the following months, my mind circled back to it, going over it again and again with the added context of everything that has happened since. I'll probably continue to do so for years. Going over scenarios, wondering what I could have done differently.

It's hard to give your past self some slack. It's hard to not hope your future self will be better. I keep hoping I would do things differently if I ever found myself in a similar situation again. To actually try to help. To do something, anyway. But I'm not sure. Instead I doubt myself, self-lacerate because I had such selfish piece of shit thoughts at the time and had acted so indifferently to him. I'm still unsure if I've changed at all from the person I was.

I've found better hearts in everyone else who felt the ripples of what happened. Maybe they too would have been as unhelpful as I was, but then again, maybe not.

I'm always doubting, but out of everything in my life, this single incident has left me more confused and sad and lonely and angry than I'd ever felt before.

Writing about it seems to have helped others, seems to have given them an outlet for otherwise inexpressible emotions. It's less to make sense of the events—that isn't the trouble. I know what happened. It's more a matter of releasing this from my memory. Putting it out into the ether. So I'm writing this now as a form of exorcism. I hope you'll understand. I'm writing to you, to a new friend, not because I think I'll actually show you, but because it helps to feel like it's directed at someone. Like it's a gift.

What happened was this:
Dennis killed himself two days later.
Jules, true to form, vanished from my life.

2 – When ripples become waves

"You mean you'd never let a guy fuck you?" Gabriel asked.

"I mean I can't really say it's on the agenda…"

"C'mon. It's something you quasi-bi guys especially should try at least once. In the name of social progress."

"Are you invalidating my identity, Gabe?" I asked.

"I merely want you to explore the full spectrum of bisexual possibility."

I scratched the back of my neck.

"The concept's just never appealed to me."

"Well, in a few years you'll be more open-minded."

"I wouldn't bet on it, Gabe."

We walked along a creek in the middle of nowhere. Gabriel guided me through the night.

"There's this really cool bridge," he explained. "Just come with me."

I didn't know what else to do except continue to resign myself to his impulses. He was experiencing a sorrow beyond my understanding, something my sympathy could never appreciate. He had an emotionally driven and pointless plan and he wanted me to be a part of it. That was all I needed to know, all the motivation required.

I didn't plan on going to Dennis' memorial service, though I entertained the idea when they first publicized the event. Most people were going because they felt like they needed to offer their support. Suicide rings far and wide wherever it takes place. They felt like they needed to rally together as a "community." But I didn't feel like I was part of that community. Or maybe, I questioned the concept of widespread community as it relates to death. Death seemed to me something best privately contemplated. Alone or in small groups of close loved ones. Making such a fuss and gathering everybody together seemed to miss the point somehow. Not to say I know the "right" way to mourn. I guess we all cope differently.

So much of me wanted to go, given the chance that Jules might show up, which I hated myself for, but couldn't deny. She hadn't been returning my calls or texts—which, truth be told, wasn't that different from normal, but she hadn't shown up at school either. Of course, going to the service just to see Jules also didn't seem right. So I couldn't think of any good reason to go. At first, I decided not to, convinced myself that the most respectful thing was to let it be. If this evening was meant for friends and family, one less stranger might be for the best. Thin the crowd, dampen the noise.

Then Gabriel—my dear, horrible, confusing friend Gabriel—called.

"I wanna go," he said. "I need to go. But I can't go by myself. I can't be that guy."

"That guy?"

He didn't elaborate.

"C'mon man, please."

We went back and forth. I insisted he explain his reasons. He insisted it was a necessity for him. The reasons were beside the point. He pleaded with me. Gabriel—who once convinced me to make out with him in a crowded room at a party when we were sixteen, causing me to spend the rest of junior year attempting to restore the fact among my peers that I was into girls too, and somehow I still didn't regret doing it—could be persuasive. It didn't take long for me to give in.

"Great!" he said, his tone changing from angry pleading to agreeably sweet. "Thanks man. I'll pick you up in a bit."

We arrived in the auditorium a few minutes late. Took two seats a few rows behind everybody else. A dozen rows were filled up in the front, a few more sprinkled with people behind them. No sign of Jules. The lights were dimmed, the principal spotlighted on stage. A tall, broad-shouldered man who nevertheless gave off the impression of a spineless bureaucrat, he stood in front of the microphone stand, which he hadn't extended enough to get the microphone close to his mouth. As we took our seats, he paused his solemn, platitude-filled speech about the fragility of life to work out how to raise the stand to his height.

"In times like these," he continued, after a blare of feedback, "we must come together as a community in order to recognize that every life is precious, and from this tragedy, we must find a lesson..."

I looked to Gabriel, who rolled his eyes and audibly groaned.

When the principal finished, he encouraged kids to step up to the mic.

"Speak up," he said. "Please. This is a difficult time for all of us, but know that you are not alone."

Slowly, mostly in groups, students began to take the stage. Most admitted that they were not close friends, merely close enough to feel burdened by the death. Fellow orchestra members, elementary school classmates, astronomy club members. Some who didn't hang out with him in real life much, but sometimes talked to him on social media. Some he had just recently befriended. A couple girls, his closest friends, they said, who managed through tears to comment on how happy he had always seemed, how they wished they could have done something to help him. They couldn't stop crying. The audience waited uncomfortably, until one of the girls set the microphone back in its stand, and they skittered off stage and sat back down.

One boy hopped on stage and played a sentimental pop song with his acoustic guitar. The performance was met with a strange, uneven round of applause.

Then a local Protestant priest gave a sermon about life and death. I kept viewing this from Jules' perspective. I kept thinking how Jules would've hated him. She would have found his sermon tacky, little more than an advertisement for his religion. He seemed so removed from the tragedy. Everybody else had at least a passing connection to Dennis. Who was this fucking guy? He even began by saying "While I never knew the young man…"

About the time he encouraged us to join in prayer for the healing power of our lord Jesus Christ, Gabriel grabbed my arm and pulled me toward the exit.

I followed Gabriel to his car. He stood along the driver's side and breathed in heavily. He looked down for a moment, slid his hand into his pocket, came up wearing brass knuckles, then slammed his fist into the car to his left, rammed it into a side window in a frantic swoop, cracking the glass. He kicked and jabbed and elbowed the passenger's side door and window until it was all banged up and the glass shattered, cursing, "FUCK! FUCK! FUCK YOU! FUCK YOU! FUCK—PIECE OF SHIT! FUCK YOU!" He took the rear view mirror in both hands and snapped it off, smashing it on the sidewalk.

Leaning up against the stranger's car, he took out a pack of cigarettes and a lighter from his jacket pocket. He lit up, hands bruised and bloodied and shaking, and puffed away at it.

"It's not right," Gabriel said. "It's not good enough."

He got in his car and slammed the door shut.

I could have left him there. Had I been in the mood for self-preservation, I probably would have. But Dennis and all the events following had left me in a state I didn't want to explore. I wanted to worry about Gabriel's issues as a means of avoiding my own.

I considered writing a note to the damaged vehicle's owner and tucking it under a windshield wiper, but thought better of it when I realized it was a Tesla. Then I joined Gabriel in his car.

He sped out of the parking lot, blowing through the next two intersections and disobeying every stop and yield sign. The stereo was booming some volatile pop-punk song. Power chords and high-pitched vocals quaked the car.

Gabriel took in cigarette after cigarette. I tried to get him to at least let me light them for him—god forbid the concept of "stopping the car"—so he could focus on the road. He would hear none of it. I just sat there in the passenger's seat, muscles tense, ready to pounce on the wheel or tuck and roll out the door.

We screeched to a halt at his house, miraculously unscathed. He opened the garage door with the remote attached to the visor, jumped out of the car, ran into the garage, and appeared again a little later with a cardboard box in his arms.

"Open the trunk, please," he said.

I pulled the latch under the driver's seat. He tossed the box inside, slammed the trunk shut and got back in. He turned down the stereo.

"Sorry," he told me, coughing into his fist, then wiping his mouth on his sleeve.

"What's in the box?"

"Flares."

"Flares? Where did you get flares?"

"You know my dad's a cop. Come on, I've got an idea. Are you with me?"

"What's the idea?"

"I just wanna go to a place. Don't worry, nothing dangerous. Promise."

Without waiting for my response, he drove us fast and reckless out of town and into the farmlands. Away from streetlights and buildings, away from the high school, away from all those guilty souls mourning together for a boy they hardly knew.

Outside now in the middle of nowhere, Gabriel continued smoking his cigarettes, almost done with the pack and almost assuredly fighting off nausea. He left a trail of butts in the wet grass and gravel like bread crumbs. Sometimes, he didn't even wait to burn them to the filter, just snuffed them out when he felt like it, on

Bryan Cebulski

tree trunks or on the ground beneath his leather soles.

We walked fast. I carried the box of flares. He held a flashlight. The path was straight and narrow. He walked a few steps ahead of me. He talked at random, things that came to his mind, sad or silly things.

Gay sex versus straight sex. Guys he'd hit on.

Shitty TV shows he couldn't help watching religiously. Absurdism.

"Have you read *The Myth of Sisyphus*?" he asked, apparently done pressing me with questions about my sexual preferences.

"Uh... I've heard of it. Albert Camus. Why?"

"It's funny. Somewhere in there, it answers why suicide isn't legitimate—even in a world without eternal values or meanings or anything. I keep reading it, even though I don't understand it. I don't know if it's just the translation's bad or I'm not smart enough or I have the attention span of a rodent, but I just can't get through it."

"Well, have you learned anything from it so far?"

"I guess I haven't killed myself yet, there's that..." He trailed off, then pointed ahead with the flashlight. "Anyway, here's the bridge!"

It popped up from the depths of the night with a flick of Gabriel's wrist. The bridge was fairly wide, made up of wooden planks, thick rusty metal support beams, and thick rusty metal railings. Gabriel walked to the middle, stood there and looked down at the running water. The noise of the water somehow accentuated the eerie nighttime quiet.

I put the box down. Gabriel tossed me the flashlight. I grabbed it and shined it in his direction. He took a flare from the box, pulled off the cap, twisted the tip, and struck the flare against the cap's rough striking surface. The flare burst bright white and red. He held the stick over the water in a shredded fist, letting the sparks fly and fall.

Then Gabriel turned to me.

"You know I never even knew Dennis, right?"

This had occurred to me. I didn't know everything about my friend though, so it was still possible.

"I didn't want to say anything," I said.

"Yeah. I didn't know Dennis. Never talked to him in my life. Saw him sometimes. Knew he existed. But I never talked to him. Not once. But I tell you, I knew Dennis. The moment the gossip on why he did it started. You know what I mean?"

"Because he was gay too?"

"Gay or whatever. Yeah, of course. But deeper. I just get kids like Dennis. I can't explain it. I know I'll regret never actually meeting him. I could have helped him. I know I'm not worth a damn, but kids like Dennis have potential. And I know that crying in a fucking high school auditorium isn't good enough to honor him. Not for me. When a person dies, things shouldn't be proper. I wanna open wounds and act on impulses and do crazy shit."

Gabriel chucked the flare into the river. It plopped into the shallow water, a tiny, strong light shining. I wondered how it worked, how a submerged flame kept burning. Some kind of oxidizer in there, I guessed. He took another flare from the box.

"I've wanted to do this for so long," he said. "I don't know why, but I've just wanted to do this. I thought the flares would look like stars."

I leaned over the railing to admire the lonely flickering red dot rippling in the water.

"It kind of does," I said.

"Yeah." Gabriel lit the second flare. The tip sparked, ignited, hissed. "This town, man... it's, I don't know. It's fine. But it's oppressive all the same, somehow. There are places with like, annual events to scare kids straight. Where you're told wanting to suck a dick is the devil possessing your body. And I guess I should be thankful I don't live in a place like that." He hurled the flare farther than the first. It splashed into the water, the hiss fading.

Gabriel started on another flare. He ripped it off the striking surface and threw it right as it began to ignite. Three lights burned bright in the water.

"But still," he went on, "do you know how much it pains me to know stuff like that legitimately happens? And how little places like where we live do anything to stop it? I mean, why would I want to live in a world where that sort of thing happens; where we're just indifferent to it, just go 'Ope, sorry, not our business' and turn our backs? It's not even scary anymore. It's just comical."

He lit and tossed another. Four drowning stars.

I bent down and took a flare for myself. It wouldn't light at first. After a few strikes, the flame shot forth, spraying molten debris onto my shirt. I let it fly and fall into the water near one side of the river, almost ashore.

We proceeded to ignite and throw the whole box into the creek. There must have been at least thirty. They joined the moon in illuminating the night, giving some clarity to the bottom of this shallow water.

When there was only one left to go, Gabriel took his last two cigarettes and gave one to me. He lit the flare and held it up between us. He put the cigarette between his lips and leaned in toward the flame. The cigarette now lit, he leaned back and started smoking. He looked back at me expectantly. I followed his actions, putting the cigarette between my lips, making sure not to actually breathe in. Gabriel rolled his eyes at me in a faux-fussy manner, fully aware of the trick.

I lay my hand down on the railing and let the cigarette burn. Then Gabriel got into a stance, pulled his arm back, and clumsily hurled the final flare. It fell, brighter than the rest, among its dying brethren.

"I guess I feel spiritually obliged to keep living for Dennis and those kids," Gabriel said. "As stupid as it sounds. If there's no reason to live, there might as well be no reason to die."

"It's a start," I said.

Gabriel shrugged and flicked his cigarette away. I did the same, glad to be rid of it.

We walked back to the car. I held the flashlight. Gabriel had this strangely mischievous smile on his face. I didn't know what he was feeling and I felt too weird myself to make any guesses.

Gabriel might have had a dark outlook, but he did mean well. He wasn't a bad person for lashing out and speaking his mind more than most people did. It was just the only way he knew how to act. He hurt you if he knew you could handle it and, however you felt about it, he never hurt without reason.

The car was parked between two trees off to the side of the road. Gabriel got in before me. The engine huffed. He turned on the headlights. I went to open the passenger's side door. It was locked. I knocked on the window.

Gabriel got back out of the car and looked at me from across the roof. He put his hands together, set them down and rested his chin in them.

"I'm jealous as hell of all those kids," he said. "They don't have to deal with this misery ever again. But still, I'm one thousand times more jealous of you. The struggle is over for them. There never was any struggle for you."

"What're you getting at?" I asked.

"You should be glad I gave you the flashlight, is all!"

He got back into the car and pressed on the stereo. Power chords rang out. The repetitive bass made the ground tremble. A screechy voice wailed. Gabriel swung the car onto the road and I heard him yell, "See ya at school!" before zooming away across miles and miles of flat unpeopled farmland.

The sound of insects buzzing filled the air. Crickets called to me. I looked up at the moon, only partially full, its color a dull gray. It was getting cold now. Dumbstruck and suddenly so self-aware, I set out on my long walk home.

After a minute or two, I started to laugh. And for whatever reason, I couldn't stop.

3 – A story often of love

Jules dropped out of school for the year and fled the country. She signed up with an organization that sets its members up with jobs on collaborating European organic farms, stores, and restaurants, to help pay for their travels. She spent a good portion of her savings on the membership fee and a plane ticket, exchanged the rest for euros, got her passport, packed a backpack, and ran off telling almost nobody. I only found this information out by approaching her little brother Joshua after school one day.

"She sorta snapped," he explained. "Screamed at our mom about how she *had* to leave. She'd already filled out all the paperwork, probably the minute she turned eighteen. I guess she's been planning this for a while. Maybe planned on going next summer. But she made a call so they could sandwich her in with a group headed for France a couple weeks ago."

"Well... Know how long she'll be gone?"

He shook his head.

"No. Doubt she'll be back soon though. The trips don't have a set deadline. You can keep on with the place you're working at for as long as you want or as long as they can keep you, and when you're ready to move on or go home, they set it up for you. I feel like once Jules is there, she won't wanna come back for a looong time."

"Yeah I can see that," I agreed, trying to hide the defeat in my voice. "You worried?"

"Eh. Not really, not for her anyway. You?"

It took a second.

"No. I guess I'm not either."

He nodded in reply, seemed to not want to discuss the matter any further.

"Well, thanks," I said. "Keep me updated."

"Sure thing."

Gabriel and I hadn't talked since that night. I saw him on occasion, smoking in the parking lot or if we crossed paths in the hallway. Incidental stuff. He was nice to me and I was nice back, but there was just a barrier between us. We talked once or twice a week, avoided the subject of that night, but the words didn't come easy anymore. Like we'd lost our understanding somewhere along the line. I didn't resent him for abandoning me and he knew that. But an inconsistency emerged, like he had tuned himself to one frequency and I to another.

I occupied my time working long hours at Hyde's Place, washing dishes and cleaning tables at night. It wasn't fun—like most menial chores, it was merely laborious and distracting. The constant stream of work and Gordon's long-winded stories kept me from thinking too much.

When I had the free time, I would make an effort to painstakingly go through my homework. Not for a love of learning, just to further distract myself. Distraction was the key. Distractions kept my feelings at bay. The exploration of one's feelings, I decided long ago, could be a noble pursuit, but it wasn't for me. Not right now.

I wanted to read more, but it was hard to focus when I sat down with a book. My state of mind wasn't right. It took no more than two or three pages before my head sunk inward toward all that stuff I wanted to avoid. For some reason though, I developed this fixation on F. Scott Fitzgerald. I picked up *The Beautiful and Damned* and found I could not put it back down. Something about the privilege and the misery of the rich. How strange and soft their lives are. I borrowed every book the local library had of his work and, when I was up to reading, which wasn't terribly often granted everything else I was going through, I committed myself to working my way through them. Often with a suitably fancy cocktail on the end table next to me.

I wanted to work out more, but whenever I set aside the time, the ability to exert energy just wasn't in me. Pride in physical appearance used to be the drive, but without Jules around, the motivation shriveled. I settled on slow jogs or easy weights with low reps with the TV on in the background, which of course meant I ended up watching TV more than working out.

In effect, this time I'd set aside for cultural refinement and physical improvement was taken up instead by idle masturbation and halfhearted exercise. I didn't feel unproductive or unhappy, all things considered. Just half-dead.

No doubt if I'd continued down this path of lackluster habits and emotional repression, I would have snapped sometime mid-December. While I like to think I have a pretty good sense of self-discipline, it can only carry a person so far by itself. The lack of company cemented into a heavy weight. Manageable to shoulder for a while, yet noticeably slipping.

My extended family and I don't communicate as often as we'd like. Cousins pop up online with a comment or question every now and then, and this one uncle is devoted to emailing us memes and satirical articles on a weekly basis, but we only get together on special occasions, the pool of which decreases yearly. With everybody getting older and busier, we've grown apart. Our schedules had become complicated, and the amount of days when we were all available and willing to travel had lessened to a thin few.

We did make an effort for occasions with food and gifts though. Thanksgiving usually had a good turnout, with everybody gathering at my grandmother's house after she'd spent the day in the kitchen preparing an always top-notch feast. Thanksgiving would then warm us up for Christmas, the big holiday. For this we'd routinely wind up at my father's fanciest establishment, The Fountain. We'd all bring a different dish to share, and then head to the banquet hall to eat, drink, and open presents all night.

But while all well and good on their own, these holidays still paled in comparison to our weddings. And my cousin Pauline just so happened to be tying the knot over New Year's Eve. We had other plans and responsibilities, but dropped, covered, or otherwise rescheduled everything to make it.

Pauline and her fiancé chose a hotel in downtown Madison for their venue. I'll spare you the details of the wedding itself. I see weddings—most weddings, anyway—as only important to people who're close to the bride and groom. Otherwise, it's just two strangers kissing in front of a trellis.

My cousin Jonathan buddied up with me for the night, first sitting next to me through the service and dinner and then supplying me with alcohol from the open bar during the reception. We danced and drank, going from champagne to shots to mixed drinks, until "Apache (Jump On It)" came on, which is around when my stomach got queasy and I settled on water. Jonathan stuck to beer.

At some point, we wandered downstairs to the hotel lobby. He stopped and talked to everyone who passed by, holding his hand out to shake, saying "Hey how's it going?" and "How's your night?" Some simply ignored him, while others shook his hand and conducted surprisingly good conversations. He spotted two attractive older women near the elevators and tried to hit on them, only to have them laugh us off and walk away.

"DAMMIT," he roared.

The receptionist looked over at him.

They made eye contact.

"DON'T JUDGE ME," Jonathan continued to shout, pointing furiously.

Meanwhile, the alcohol was having a weird introspective effect on me. Drunkenness doesn't always work the way it's supposed to, filling your heart with merriment and joy. Sometimes, it has that way of highlighting your worst thoughts instead. Things I wouldn't have ordinarily let myself feel, perspectives I wouldn't have ordinarily taken. My subconscious was on the prowl for reasons to hate myself.

You don't even know Pauline, do you? She's related by blood, but you know nothing about her. What's your problem, man? What makes you think you belong here?

You are nothing but a drunken, overprivileged fool.

Jules is gone. The only person you've given any real amount of attention to for the past few months of your life has up and vanished, and now you've got nobody.

You literally have no friends anymore. You are at the bottom of the social barrel. You could vanish tomorrow and nobody would notice.

"I'M GONNA THROW UP," Jonathan shouted. He stood there a few seconds, letting those strangers' eyes cast their glances at this one-man fiasco. Then, as if it were nothing, he waddled into the restroom. I followed.

He puked into one of the urinals for some reason, desperately pulling the level over and over, expecting it to flush. It only made the shallow bowl overflow and cake his black leather shoes with chunky orange water.

For a few minutes, Jonathan leaned over the poorly chosen vomit-vessel, regurgitating the contents of his stomach. I gave him paper towels, which he dropped to the floor and stomped on instead of using to wipe his mouth.

Having adequately trashed this area, Jonathan slid toward the sinks and ducked his head under one of the faucets. It was an automatic. After feeling around for the handle, he saw the sensor and began to finger it. The water shot out in haphazard spurts. This went on longer than I probably should have let it.

Jonathan and I ran up and down State Street, shouting and cheering for the new year. People hooted along with us; partiers and vagrants, people on their post-bar trek home, people who simply felt like wandering the streets on this soothingly lukewarm winter eve.

If we were annoying, we didn't notice.

We ran into five of Jonathan's fraternity brothers. Each clasped hands and half-hugged him. They asked us where we were going. Before we could answer, one yelled "DUDE, LET'S RACE," and took off toward the capitol building. One followed, then another, and soon all seven of us were sprinting.

We reached the capitol square and made our way down the boulevard toward the lake, and eventually found ourselves in front of Monona Terrace, completely winded. I tasted metal in my mouth. A couple minutes passed as we tried to catch our breath.

"Some girl gave me head here one time!" Jonathan told us, his voice wishing to tell the world. "IT WAS—ahem. It was about this time of night. She was really into doin' it in public places."

"Was that Cassandra?" someone asked.

"It was totally Cassandra!"

"What a hoe! Show me where!"

They blocked the terrace off at night, but we jumped the barriers and dashed toward the edge overlooking the lake. I stood there mesmerized by the winter wind and the dark waves as Jonathan showed his friends the spot where he had received open-air fellatio.

"Oh fuck you, man! That's barely public," somebody yelled. "Who the hell's going to notice you there?"

"Fine, asshole, I'll get my dick sucked at Starbucks next time!"

I took a seat on a metal patio chair, closed my eyes, breathed. The sound of water was nice. As fun as they were, the bros didn't suit me. I phased them out soon enough. The world spun—not too much, but just enough to make me not want to move an inch.

I thought to overcome this dizzy spell through sheer willpower, as if that were possible. I smiled and breathed and breathed and breathed, paying attention to nothing except the sound of waves and wind and the rising and falling of my chest. I wanted to be sad. I couldn't remember the last time I had cried and, all of a sudden, I wanted to cry. But I was too sick. Too aware of the presence of those guys. The only thing I could afford to think about was my breathing.

Time grew fuzzy.

Some time later, a soft glow penetrated my eyelids, breaking me from that inward regression.

"So it is you!" a voice called.

I opened my eyes. They placed one hand gently on my shoulder, then with the other, used their cellphone to illuminate their face.

"Can ya see me?"

It took a minute. From that angle, in my state, at this time of night, it was hard to tell anything apart. The silhouettes of garbage cans and fire hydrants could look as much like a person as a real human from the right distance.

I pulled myself up by the railing and turned around to get a better look at them. They beamed at me, bright white teeth and dark brown skin.

"Oh! Heeeeey!" I slurred.

It was Estelle—new name pending, they'd announced on social media a few months back, still working out the options—someone who I'd gone to school with since kindergarten. Not friends, really. That uncertain relationship between two people who grew up in the same community without really ever forming a bond. Except that little bit of history, but, well...

"I thought that was you," they said cheerfully.

"You did? How?"

"I have night vision, you didn't know that?"

"I did not know that," I deadpanned.

They bumped me with their elbow.

"Anyway, what'cha up to in Madison?"

I explained about the wedding and everything.

"We're just... uh. I dunno what we're doing now. You?"

"New Year's party with the fam! My cousins are over there palin' with your boyfriends."

"Jumped the barriers too?"

"Uh-huh. Well how y'like that? What're the odds eh?"

Estelle and I didn't have a warm history, to tell the truth. They hadn't even crossed my mind much for the past couple years. And I doubt I crossed theirs. It was more the excitement of seeing a familiar face in an unfamiliar place that brought out those tender vibes between us.

Our groups merged. The boys and girls, drunk and competitive as they were, cheerfully chided and flirted with each other. There were two fewer girls, but they'd already decided their partners for the night, leaving two college bros behind. Funny how much faster these things happen when you're drunk.

Estelle and I watched, commenting on how our

groups got on, critiquing the couples. I didn't know any of Jonathan's friends, but gave my rough judgments anyway. I concluded that probably none of them were to be trusted with Estelle's relatives, including Jonathan. Estelle shrugged it off.

"They're tough girls," they said. "And your boys seem like harmless jackasses. Nah, they'll be fine."

This suggested to me that we were going to part from their company. Then I realized we already had. My guys and their girls had jumped the barrier out of the terrace and were hooting their way up the boulevard. A couple of the bros were singing "Ain't No Mountain High Enough" to the girls' slightly bemused disapproval. Estelle and I looked at each other and giggled.

"Well," I said, "what should we do?"

"Ohhh I don't know. Let's hang here for now. We can catch up or something."

"Sounds good."

The terrace finally gained that sense of tranquility I'd been after. Empty public places have that effect. Having so much space to yourself, knowing that we're the only two souls warming this place. Estelle placed their elbows, padded with a wool jacket, on the railing and put their knuckles under their chin.

"Such a weird night," they said, as much to themself as to me.

"I've been meaning to ask you... do you, uh, do you still hate me?" It was a question I had been wanting to ask, though truth be told, mostly I hoped I would just never have to face Estelle ever again. "Because of back then and all."

They shrugged.

"No, not really. You turned yourself around."

"Still, I never apologized or anything."

"It is what it is. I haven't thought about it much, honestly."

"Could I make up for it somehow?"

"Dude, as far as I'm concerned, it happened between two entirely different people."

I should explain. In another place and in another time, your humble narrator was what we call an incorrigible asshole.

Not so much during my childhood—I was a pretty decent kid—but from about eleven to fifteen-years-old. Those woebegone days of adolescent insecurities and the chaotic ego. Sometime early into my second decade I developed a superiority complex. Maybe it was misguided soul-searching, a wish to seek a definite identity, however cruel it might be. Maybe it was a simple case of peer pressure.

My friends were the snobby, condescending type. Products of a high class upbringing. We didn't bully so much as casually patronize and belittle peers from a distance. Put ourselves up on a pedestal and watched the laymen struggle beneath our dangling feet. Only associated with a select group of people, spending most of our time audibly judging others, making them feel like crap. You know. Real *Mean Girls* shit.

Now, this incorrigible asshole became somebody's object of affection. They were a chubby, socially deprived preteen. The two had social studies together and had assigned seats next to each other. The asshole was nice to them because he figured they would do most of the work on group projects. But they took it as flirtation and began to engage him in—late night text messages, talking to him in the hallways, trying to walk home with him after school.

He didn't respond to the texts and went out of his way to avoid them during and after school. They didn't pick up on these hints. They started asking him if he could be their boyfriend. Just like that, two or three times a day for a week. Internet, cellphone, face-to-face. They had to have an answer. They didn't seem to know any better. He avoided answering each time, logging off, not responding, walking away.

When they wouldn't stop, the boy retaliated by spreading rumors. Rumors involving acts of self-pleasure with certain phallic vegetables. The boy was respected by his peers. His word became the truth without question.

That insecure preteen consequently faced the brunt of an immense wave of ridicule, which lasted for the rest of the year. Friends dropped away, too embarrassed to be around them. People they did not even know teased them while passing by in the hall. One day, they inquired as to the origin of the rumors, which eventually led them to the boy. Hurt terribly, they approached him at his locker after school one day, and asked if he had really fabricated such horrible things. The boy, at the breaking point, did not make eye contact, but very loudly called them a psycho bitch and told them to leave him alone forever. And that was the last time they spoke.

I hadn't thought much about that incident since then. Once I cultivated myself out of that snobbish miasma, I regretted it, but the two of us had never made amends. I was never driven to check up on them or anything. They seemed to have grown up fine. Got new friends. Explored their identity. Discovered online queer communities, if their social media was any judge. Managed to help develop our high school's Black student union, despite pushback from its administration.

The rumor faded as rumors do. They grew into their body, gained better friends, and self-assurance. My cruel act seemed so insignificant compared to the person they'd become. I justified myself by thinking that it wouldn't have made a difference to ask forgiveness.

That it would only reopen old wounds.

After the night's meanderings, we ended up in my hotel room. It didn't take much of a push on my part—they seemed oddly happy to hang with me. In fact, I don't think I even did much encouraging. My hotel room was merely the place to go, no decision about it, nothing suggestive suggested. I told them I had a room to myself since my father was staying with his girlfriend and the rest of my family's rooms were full. They thought it was the coolest thing to have a hotel room to ourselves. And better still, it housed the leftover beer and wine coolers from our post-rehearsal dinner party last night.

Estelle and I lay on the bed an appropriate distance apart, sipping wine coolers and watching late-night reruns of *Friends*. The arrangement was curiously domestic, especially how we talked. It wasn't deep or confiding or special. Just two people in a room together. It felt very comfortable at the time.

"Who's your favorite friend?" I asked.

Estelle shrugged.

"I guess Phoebe since she's weird and plays guitar. But I don't know. I never really watched this show, to be honest. You?"

"Hm. I don't know if have one either."

"My guess was going to be Ross."

"I've never been so insulted! I'd like to be Monica if anyone."

"You're not enough of a control freak. I like her less than Ross."

"Fascinating," I said, smirking. "Well what kinds of characters do you like?"

"Oh, I'm all about 'the bitch who develops a heart of gold' types. Cordelia in *Buffy*, Whitley in *A Different World*. You know?"

"Ah yeah, those two are good. Why that type though?"

"Because they're good people, but they don't bull-shit around. They say and do what they want and leave anything they don't. I don't know, I guess I admire something about that."

I nodded and let the conversation linger there. We laughed along with the canned audience. Long stretches of time went by without conversation.

During a commercial break, we started to make out. Just because, I guess. Beforehand, we had given each other a look, casually turning our heads toward each other. Eyes met, acknowledged, agreed, and kissing ensued.

It lasted approximately a minute, about as long as the commercial break. They broke from me in an instant and we went right back to watching. I was drunk and exhausted so I wasn't too beat up about it, but it still confused me. I looked at them again. They looked as if it had never happened. I couldn't ask.

Estelle decided to leave around sometime well after midnight. They hopped out of bed and told me they should be heading out.

"Bye," I said.

They gave me another kiss, then gave my left cheek a gentle slap.

"Keep in touch back home, eh?"

I nodded.

They skipped out of the room.

The door shut behind them with a satisfying click.

I was alone. I looked around—at the cooler half-empty with bottles of thinly alcoholic drinks, at the popcorn texture of the ceiling, at the drapes, at the darkness beyond the windows, at *Friends* playing on the TV.

I was being a miserable asshole, I decided. There was not a single thing in my life to complain about. Stupid to even consider being sad.

I promptly fell asleep.

4 – Gabriel's letter, or shit fuck nothing makes sense

(The following was found stuffed into my mailbox on Sunday morning. I say morning, though more likely it was placed there the night prior. I have no way to prove this, aside from how I woke up in the middle of the night to a crashing noise and found someone had thrown a large rock at my bedroom window, leaving a fine, distinct spiderweb crack in the center of the pane. Shortly after this, I heard a car engine gun to life and roar away from my otherwise quiet suburban street.

The letter was handwritten, chaotically folded, practically crushed, and stuffed into a manila envelope.

I haven't seen Gabriel since.)

Straight guys get all offended when I hit on them. That pisses me off. It's insecurity, isn't it? They aren't comfortable with their sexuality. They're afraid of being thought of as gay when they're not. It should be a "Thanks, but no thanks dude," not a "Fuck off I'm not gay! How could you even think that?!" I will apologize if your sexual orientation is not what I'd hoped, but raging at me is just making it that much more difficult for me to find someone. It's tough enough for a straight guy to successfully find a straight girl. I've got these hurdles of bullshit to leap over before I can even get to that stage.

I guess it's a solid ice breaker though.

"Do you like cock?" "Yeah!" "Woah, me too!"

And while I'm gear grinding, why do so many people refuse to believe bisexuality exists? Why wouldn't it exist? I mean surely it's not a half-and-half tie—but things aren't as black and white as we'd like them to be. I, for one, think there's only bisexuality; working on different levels, and some levels don't always have to involve orgasm.

I guess bisexuality doesn't occur to most people. They either don't experience the feeling or bury it away. But we ought to be comfortable doing whatever with whomever regardless of the organs you find between their legs. Remove gender roles and remove labels. Gotta get rid of that negative stigma attached to plowing dudes, being plowed by them. We're cool with girls experimenting, but it's major taboo with guys. The possibility of being even slightly homoerotically-inclined freaks the fuck out of straight guys. It might be okay to be gay nowadays, but it's still an insult to be viewed as gay in the straight community. Isn't it healthy to explore our options, though? Hell, not even explore, just to know it's there and it's not wrong. Even if we fall in love with the preferred gender in the long run; even if we don't experiment with the unpreferred gender at all, we'd all be better off appreciating the possibility without repercussion.

That's what I say to get bicurious guys into bed, anyway. And I do have a fairly good track record there. You know me. If nothing else, I can be smooth with tipsy boys. It's probably more fun than it should be. Not that I should feel bad. Or in rare cases, too bad. Even if they freak out afterwards, it's nothing they didn't want real bad at the time. Some, if I'm lucky, have a good time and come back for more. Some remain relatively chill, understand it was a curious fling and move on. Others become troubled. I try to be reasonable and help out, keep tabs on them, make sure they get back into the flow of being a dumb straight boy. Most do and probably block out the experience in the process. "Boy was I drunk last night!" One time a guy had to go to therapy. That riles me. Come on, dude. Maybe it was weird, a bit too new, but don't tell me it wasn't fun. It was a one-time thing. 99% straight is still acceptable. You can go back to fucking girls. The universe will understand.

Casual sex doesn't gratify me in any deep way. All the same, it would be a lie to say it's not fun. Everybody needs a goal, yeah, but more importantly, everybody needs something to amuse himself with in the meantime. And as annoying as straight guy insecurities can be, I'm not sensitive to rejection, and hitting on guys is entertaining. If my pursuits are fruitful... well, don't even get me started. Suffice it to say, it's wonderful.

Dating is nice. I do have feelings beyond rage and horniness somewhere. It's nice to have someone to confide in. The paranoia is too much for me though. I can handle the rejection of strangers, but I can't handle the rejection of somebody who means something to me.

Maybe that in part explains why I've been avoiding you. I mean, I trust you. Might even like you. Not that you're romantically appealing. You're just a person who's easy to get along with. Good at withholding judgments until you've assembled the facts. You follow a code. And you have respect. Respect even for assholes like me. And you seem conscious of not taking your privileges for granted. I hate you for your privileges and well, I've expressed that, but you honestly do seem to try your best to appreciate them. And you like listening. That might actually be all it is. You like learning about other people. Who else does that?

I had a serious boyfriend once. Kind of a boyfriend anyway. "Boyfriend" demeans the relationship's depth. His name was—well, is—Tate. A four letter name. A unique one. The kind of name you think they reserve for babies. I can't imagine anybody else over the age of six named Tate.

Indulge me in a how-we-met story. I'll keep it short. It wasn't much of a meeting anyway. He moved here from California when we were in eighth grade. (You didn't go to my middle school, so you wouldn't have known him.) It was, among other things, a church-related decision. His parents no longer approved of the way theirs was operating. Tate told me a newly transferred priest semi-successfully encouraged his flock not only to tolerate, but to even support, certain minority rights. So they decided to move out here. Our town is lenient on a lot of minor misdemeanors, like your notorious alcoholism, but you must admit we have a little too much Bible-thumping. I guess Tate's family digs that though. A friend recommended the area. The parents checked it out, were swooned since we're really good at selling whatever image the real estate market requires. They sold their house, bought a new one, reestablished their careers (they both worked for the same nationwide company, easy transfers I guess), and made the move in almost no time at all.

Tate, an only child, didn't have a say in the decision.

I don't know about you, but I can never remember how I became friends with a person. Even Tate. It just happened. Everybody did that in middle school. We saw another human being around our age and latched onto them. If we were lucky, we liked the person. If not, well, we were stuck with them, because it's too difficult to make new friends. I suppose I was one of the lucky ones.

I experienced a lot of happiness with Tate. Even if it was only for a short time. It's more than what most people get at that age.

Tate had lunch and a couple classes with me. We started sitting together and talking all the time. He must have made the first move. I didn't make any moves back then. Except to punch things.

I admit I was a bit of a dick to the kid at first. Something about him. He looked like such a weenie: scrawny and girly. Wore an acid-washed jean jacket and tight pants, and clearly spent a solid thirty minutes on his hair every morning. He stuck with me though despite my resistance. And eventually I mellowed out. Even worse: It started to feel nice and warm to be with him. I even started to *miss* him when he wasn't around.

Girls couldn't get over how adorable he was and flocked to him by the dozens. Consequently, some guys developed a passionate hatred for him. Regardless, he made friends with half the school in a matter of weeks. He was that kind of person. Beautiful, kind, social, funny, beaming. I didn't have many friends. I picked up smoking pretty early—seventh grade, I think—and my only friends were the people I smoked with, and they weren't much. For some reason, of all people, Tate picked *me* to be his special friend.

Tate's first great sin was vanity. Which was, and honestly still is, adorable. If you saw him through my eyes you could hardly blame him for being a little self-absorbed. One of his favorite hobbies was taking pictures and videos of himself. They were what you'd expect. Silly. I'd probably cringe if I saw them now. Black-and-white with his eyes colored in, over filtered. The kind of pictures and videos the internet is flooded with. I'm sure you know what I'm talking about. Irritating to everyone except teenage girls and me.

After our friendship developed for some time, we started to hang around outside school. We started to have sleepovers. Since I didn't want him staying over at my place and since his parents didn't approve of me, I would sneak into his house through the bedroom window after his parents fell asleep.

Tate always hugged me upon entering. He was an affectionate person. It occurred to me early on that this was a bit too tender a relationship for two guys. It just felt too good to question.

We spent nights talking, browsing the internet, taking pictures of each other. He had a penchant for ridiculously sweet drinks. He would warm up ice cream and drink it like hot chocolate. When I look back, it's hard to imagine we actually had anything to talk about. We had nothing in common. I guess the common ground was that we were both secretly extremely attracted to each other. And that fact alone left our conversations brimming.

The realization that maaaaybe we aren't all that straight revealed itself more tangibly when we started sleeping together. Just sleeping. My home life got to the point where most weekends I'd rather risk sneaking into Tate's than stay at my place. His bedroom was a sanctuary. The walls were painted this gentle blue and everything was soft. A glimmering sapphire in the dark. He had a walk-in closet and a huge bed decked with the fluffiest pillows. His walls were lined with posters from Brat Pack movies: *The Breakfast Club* and *St. Elmo's Fire* and *Some Kind of Wonderful*. It was so impossibly cute. Totally unlike me. I loved it. Nothing bad could happen to me in so sweet a room.

The first time we slept together, freshman year by this point (he went to some Christian academy for high school, which is, again, why you never knew him), happened after I drank too much and got into a brawl with a certain family member. I got kicked out of the house and stumbled across town to Tate's. My phone was somewhere not in my pocket so I couldn't call in advance, but I peeked into his window, saw him alone in the glow of his laptop and knocked. He jumped back in fright. Once he saw it was me, he gathered his cool and lifted the window.

"Gabe?" Man, if only you could hear his voice. The gentle rhythm of it. Made you want to squeeze him till it hurt. When he saw my beat-up face—semi-torn lip, onset of a black eye—he whimpered and went, "Oh Gabe! What happened?"

I asked if I could stay the night with him, and he popped out the screen and let me in. I climbed over and hugged him, clung to him. I was drunk and in need. He helped. It felt like the greatest thing. Beat up as I was, I felt like I had won. Nobody else had this kind of love in their life. Everything else could suck as long as I had this.

We stayed up late, not saying much, sitting on the carpet.

He cradled my head in his skinny arms. I could feel his ribs.

"I love you," I said, touching the line of his chin, staring through bleary eyes.

He smiled down at me and said, "Yeah, I love you too."

I know, I know. Fuck off, it's special to me.

We went to bed. Tate's bed is still the best bed I've ever slept in. It smelled like him, like strawberries and kiwi and green tea. I got to envelope myself in Tate's world, all its pleasant pure smells and sights and vibes. Syrupy stuff. He made me feel like the luckiest person alive.

Usually I slept on the floor—he had so many extra pillows and blankets, it was practically another bed—but from that night onward, he let me sleep with him. Tate liked me there, it was easy to tell. I'd wake up with him huddled up next to me, some part of him touching me. His head on my chest, his hand in mine.

It still hadn't occurred to us that we might be gay. Self-delusion is a funny thing. I thought I was just making use of the affection readily available to me—affection that I damn well needed regardless of who gave it. Tate probably assumed he was a naturally cuddly creature and would have been acting the same had I been a girl. We did acknowledge that we loved each other though. More nights than one would I tell him so, at varying levels of sobriety, and every time he would say the same back. We were delusional, insecure, fucked-up freshmen in high school.

Not that the delusions lasted long. A couple weekends later, we started kissing. When you're under the covers completely alone with the most beautiful person you've ever seen in your life, it's difficult not to kiss him. But with us kissing, the issue was finally unavoidable: Maaaaybe something was different with us. I'd kissed girls in middle school and it did nothing for me. I didn't get the appeal, didn't get why guys worked so furiously toward getting kissed. Tate, in short, made me understand.

I remember coming out.

I was home alone, looking at myself in the mirror.

"I'm gay," I said. Then I said it once more, then again. It was true. It made sense.

Straight guys' hearts do not melt when they kiss another guy. Straight guys do not get painful erections when they kiss another guy. I didn't beat myself up over it; it was totally fine. But my confession was missing something. Then it dawned on me.

"I'm gay and if anybody's got a problem with it, I will beat the shit out of them."

I repeated this like a mantra.

School friends already assumed I was gay, given my uncomfortably close friendship with that sissy cherub, so nothing much changed for me. I didn't go around parading my newfound self-discovery anyway. The admittance was for my personal benefit. Anybody was free to know if they asked, not that they did, and I corrected people under false assumptions ("Hey, what do you think of that girl over there?" "Well I like bangin' dudes, but she's not bad." "Oh. Wait, what?"). I just didn't make a big fuss over it. Some people need a big fuss. I'm not that guy.

Tate still wasn't quite convinced. He didn't like being

labeled gay, given his backwards Christian background. Gay meant going to hell. He didn't wholly believe in the doctrines he was brought up with, but they still nagged at him. That predetermined guilt. He didn't stand a chance against it.

Not that I'm knocking Christianity in general. It's a solid existential ethical coping mechanism for some types. But most Christians don't actually know what their religion is. They just pick and choose scripture as it suits their needs, then to hell with anybody who disagrees. That's how Tate's parents were anyway. Nice folks, as long as you were straight and white and upper class and agreed with everything their preacher told them. God forbid we ever do the research ourselves, make up our own minds.

Tate was comfortable with everything else though. He didn't mind my smoking, didn't mind drinking, didn't mind any taboo besides dudes having sex with dudes. As if the only thing the Bible says is "No homos in heaven."

Tate started to form this wacked-out concept that he wasn't gay, he just liked me. A guy. A male guy who happens to be a dude. And he couldn't help that. He wasn't hetero- or homosexual, he was Gabriel-sexual. Being Gabriel, I was semi-okay with this, but I still worried over his mental well-being. He was totally fucking gay. Everybody knew it but him.

The trouble with Tate began, really began, when he started hanging around college thespians. I'm reasonably biased, but please, for my sake, stay away from college thespians. Especially if they're named Vicki. Fucking Vicki. I'm a jealous piece of shit and I'm the first to admit it, but from the first moment, I did not trust Vicki.

Tate had been involved with school plays ever since he moved here. Fun, shitty plays. They filled up his time and they offered the kinds of carefree friendships and entertainment that I couldn't provide. He only worked crew, never performed. Strange, given his high self-image, but he couldn't commit to acting. Wracked his nerves. Too much work. Something like that. He just didn't do it.

His friends from that crowd started dipping their feet in dirty water during high school, experimenting with booze and drugs and sex. Tate didn't catch on until they found college students to party with. Like Vicki. Vicki was a freshman at a nearby public university. What kind of creepy fuck can only find high schoolers to party with, when you're a college student with your own apartment?

Tate's circle of friends started hanging with her at her place. I like to think because nobody her own age was naïve enough to give her the time of day. It was the most secure place for their newly discovered penchant for experimenting with mind-altering substances. Which Tate didn't do much of himself. He usually spent the weekends with me in mutual touchy-feely smoochy infatuation. But he did drink a little. An early bloomer maybe, but then I started even earlier, so I couldn't give him a rough time. I was uneasy with him doing this kind of thing without me around, but he'd describe his evenings to me in detail afterward. Always typical drunken revelry. Nothing bad. He tried smoking weed a couple times, liked it, but stopped, not wanting to make a habit out of it. His friends were getting into heavier substances, hippy stuff, ecstasy, but he refrained. Everybody draws the line somewhere.

Sex was the trouble. Yeah, here we go.

Tate and I made love by some definition every night for nearly two years. We had sex exactly once. Depth of contact built steadily up in the nights prior to copulation. It started out like I already described. Kissy huggy goo-goo. Then we progressed. Cuddling remained the main stimulus, but kissing evolved into heavier kissing, pajamas shed, and we became more ambitious in how and where we touched. I can't and won't exactly describe to you the first time I saw him naked. You're probably already squeamish. Pale, skinny, flat-chested probably isn't your type. But all's there is to say is that my whole being was close to exploding. We kissed each other all over the first time we were naked together. Not saying a word besides soft "I love you"s, just enjoying it, letting it happen.

We both got off, but the act of sex itself did not take place. Okay, okay. I know sex doesn't need penetration to be sex. But there was something different between how we connected that night, and how we connected the following nights.

Sex with feeling is a wonderful, wonderful thing. I feel like you're still a virgin, but goddamn I hope you get to experience it someday soon. My liaisons since my brief time with Tate have been nice, but they don't compare. It's the only time love and lust merged together for me. Lust is a bit like using; love is a bit like understanding. And so if you can understand each other well you can sure as hell use each other well. Boy oh boy, let me tell you.

The night ended in a euphoric daze. Hell, all the time we spent together was a euphoric daze. A pink cotton candy mist of human warmth under sheets soft as lotion. And I'll never get that kind of happiness again, I'm sure. And that's fine. It's enough. It's just a shame it had to end so poorly.

I found out it wasn't Tate's first time. There. It's out there. Fuck. Maybe I should have known, given the ease with which I put… well, yeah. After we did the deed, he explained it to me. He accidentally let spill why his libido had all of a sudden skyrocketed.

God, fuck. Why did I judge him so much? Why did I care? But I do. I still do.

"That was the best yet," he said, eyes closed and a smile growing on his pink lips. He meant it as a compliment, oblivious to the statement's blatant implications.

I asked him what he meant.

He got scared. Eventually I squeezed every detail out of him.

I guess sexual liberation strikes us in different ways. Some channel it into one person, bask in the sweetness, love, love, love. Others, meanwhile, get freaky.

Who the fuck am I to judge, though? I've gotten it on with more than one guy at a time before.

What the fuck is wrong with me, with this double-standard? I don't have a good answer. It's all instinctual.

It turned out Tate had a whole different life from the one he shared with me. I can be violent and depressing but damn, Tate was my beacon. He kept me going. And he kept this life from me. That's still a knife to the heart.

I wish I were tactful. I wish I had grace. But I don't and I'm a shit storyteller. This won't hit you the way it hit me. You don't know Tate. You'll never know Tate. I can't as a writer make you feel the connection with Tate that I had. Writing can only communicate so much. Sometimes if you're lucky, feelings pass through. But there were too many feelings running between Tate and me. You're not going to get it all. Or even some. But still. I have to write it down. Been letting it churn too long. Drinking early on weekdays and smoking a pack a day and punching things and manipulating insecure sixteen-year-old boys offers only a finite amount of release. I need somebody to hear me.

Vicki took a liking to Tate right off the bat. Tate liked her back. And I guess if I'm going to give her a single compliment, it would have to be on her looks. She had that chic French girl thing going for her. Black hair cut evenly in a bob. Always elegantly, darkly, simply attired. She even smoked cigarettes sometimes, through one of those black holders. It was all about image. A real class act.

I don't know how it happened. At some point though, she started casually seducing Tate. And he let it happen. He might have liked it, might have wanted it. I'm under the impression, maybe false, that he only wanted to want it. Girls usually treated Tate like a pet—this wanting to jump his bones thing was new to him. So he let her. And let. And when his little theater friends felt like joining in, he let them too. Boys and girls, whoever. Tate let things happen to him. He let them all happen to him.

Again, who am I to judge? It was probably fun. But Tate was supposed to be mine, dammit! What happened to Gabriel-sexual? What happened to homos going to hell? Was the exclusivity not clear? Did he not see sex as a natural extension of our loving each other?

Tate tried at first to tell me about his experimentation as if it were nothing. Just testing the waters. A fun way to pass the time. He knew his friends, liked his friends, fooled around with his friends. It was just for fun, for experience. But the conversation took a grim turn almost immediately. I don't remember exactly how the rest of it went, but it was something like an avalanche of questions and fury. Who the fuck does this Vicki bitch think she is? How many goddamn diseases am I going to get from you? How could you think I'd be okay with this? I fought so hard not to clasp my hands around his neck and squeeze. It was the most angry I'd ever been. Sometimes, my rage is for show, something I do to both vent and amuse. This rage began in a burst of confusion and hurt, then settled into quiet. Quiet rages are the bad ones. Quiet rage means you don't know how to react, you're taken so far aback, so in shock, so full of fury, it feels like you could burst.

Tate.

It sucks to be disgusted by the guy you used to consider the most beautiful person on the planet.

In another lifetime, maybe I beat up Tate, maybe I beat up myself, maybe I trashed the room, screamed, attacked his parents, got arrested, and then got out, only to attack Vicki and her brood next. In this lifetime, I cried. I fell to my knees at the edge of Tate's big soft bed and cried. I cried until morning. He tried consoling me, but

I threw stuff at him or knocked him away when he drew too close.

He tried justifying his actions to me. He was confused, he explained. It started as an experiment, a test of his sexual appetite, and spiraled out of control when he found he couldn't stop. He was just young and confused and needed to figure himself out, he said. He didn't know if he could stop sleeping with other people, he said. But he only loved me. He really only loved me. He didn't equate sex with love. Sex was a pastime. Maybe he would stop someday, but again, he wasn't sure if he could call it quits with his multiple partners now. He admitted that this situation was curious. But that's how it was, and he was sorry.

I mumbled something about how he was a sissy bitch slut and left. I spent the whole next day drinking and punching holes in my bedroom walls. I hardly slept for weeks.

Yes, I know I'm a parody of myself.

Tate moved soon after that. I never talked to him or saw him again. There were rumors that his parents decided to move after they found out about his secret promiscuity. I have a feeling they made him go to one of those gay rehabilitation camps. They're probably living in some sheltered fucked-up WASP suburb, even worse than ours. Maybe Tate's killed himself too.

I'm numb to the whole fiasco now. I can't remember what it was like to love a person. Maybe it would've been better to keep my composure, be considerate, when he revealed his nature to me.

No, that would've been too unlike me.

Which brings me to Dennis.

Well, not really.

But I want to talk about Dennis.

Again, you didn't know him and neither did I. But in hindsight I saw, however briefly, something of Tate in him. They were similarly sensitive young guys. Abnormal and sweet and warm and troubled. But they took two very different roads. Tate corrupted himself, Dennis ended himself. And who's to decide the correct way to cope?

I almost attempted to kill myself once. With a razor, of course. You've got to go with the most bloody option. Don't worry, I took one shallow stroke and decided I couldn't do it. Patched the wound up and went on with my life.

I told you how I'm reading that Albert Camus essay. It's still foreign to me. My understanding is marginal at best. But the myth itself keeps coming back to me. What if I'm Sisyphus? What if I'm pushing that boulder up that hill? And I keep concluding: If I'm doomed to failure and know this, then at least I'm going to find a way to enjoy myself in the meantime.

I know what I said to you before, about how if I might as well die, then I might as well live. My almost attempt may perhaps be connected to this conclusion. Dying is decidedly not for me. Too easy. I'm a small time masochist. Life is a merry-go-round of bullshit and pain and sometimes, there's a patch of mild contentment. Might as well enjoy it all while it lasts.

I've wasted enough of your time. Not that your time is so precious.

I might like to hang out with you again someday, but I'm not so sure I'll stick around this area much longer.

Maybe by the time you get this letter I'll be gone. Maybe not. Can I change my life that much? That lady friend of yours had the stones.

Till we meet again, if we meet again. I guess.

5 – Static and grain

Months after the wedding I started pondering—or musing or mulling or brooding or whatever—over Jules again, a practice that I thought I had abandoned.

This time though, I tried not to linger so much on her absence, avoided dwelling on my unrequited feelings for her or regretting my inability to actually act on them. Rather, I worked toward preparing for that faraway day when she returned. Defining who she was and could be to me. Memories—did we have so many or was I stretching out a short supply?—were stored in my head like film reels. I went to bed early every night and lay awake, staring at the black void of the ceiling, splicing the footage together.

She meant so much to me—I had to wonder why. She wasn't a part of my life long enough to make such a significant impact. I have a habit of fixating on people, I know, but these fixations don't come from nowhere.

On the other hand, my mind can latch onto concepts and illusions too easily, making someone seem more to me than they actually are. Still, surely that didn't stop Jules from being something, at least.

Though we'd gone to the same schools forever, we finally actually met properly junior year. This was the more or less perfect time, during that transitional period in my life when I was trying to suppress my former pretensions and become a better person. I was shifting my social circles, which is difficult in high school, when everybody is so afraid of breaking away from whoever they've always stuck with.

63

I noticed her, liked her, the idea of her at least, but didn't pry my way into her life until we happened to wind up at the same backyard bonfire party one weekend in the spring of my junior year.

These "bonfires"—really just a normal campfire, the setting of about three-fourths of the typical teenager's party scene where I live—worked out the same every time. They were good and bad because you knew exactly what you were getting into.

A brief lowdown: Gather as many chairs as possible, preferably lawn chairs, horribly uncomfortable of course, and set them around a fire, probably started with gasoline and wet wood that blows smoke into your face no matter where you stand. Hide the beer behind a shed or a jungle gym or some place. Hide the spirits in water bottles. Hide the weed in medicine containers and hide those in cargo pants pockets and backpacks. No need to hide cigars, swishers and vape pens really. Start drinking almost immediately. Sit back and drink watery beer. Smoke in some inconspicuous location. Proceed to get drunk, high, or both. Maybe do something stupid you'll later regret. Direct your energy toward the people you like. Talk. See if you can't find a decent conversation. You probably won't. By the end of the night, just hope it wasn't a waste of time.

I brought four bottles of an IPA to this particular gathering. The kid sitting next to me asked if he could try.

"Sure."

He took a long swig, seemed to study the flavor on his tongue for a couple seconds, swallowed, and handed it back to me.

"Eh, kinda nasty," he said. Which meant he left me with a near-full bottle with his backwash in it. I poured it out on the patchy grass.

Later that night, I saw him pouring whipped cream-flavored vodka and pineapple juice into a plastic cup, yelling, "This is the best shit!"

Now these bonfires typically take place in secluded areas, homes in the country, or at least in the peripheral neighborhoods where cops don't go patrolling. The host of this particular gathering lived in town, where the houses stood side by side, and the police station was only a few blocks away. Their backyard wasn't even fenced in. It was decidedly sketchy. Nobody was out of control, granted. We weren't loud either. You couldn't see us from the road. The only lights came from the fire and from the guys who thought they were cool smoking grape swishers by the neighbor's picket fence. But still, it was essentially out there in the open. I thought it best to only have a beer or two and leave.

Another group joined in an hour or so. Some girls. More importantly, some hot girls. It had been a so-called sausage fest for a while there.

My companions livened up at their arrival. Seating was arranged, a couple girlfriends united with their respective boyfriends, and things were all of a sudden packed around the fire.

The dynamic shifted. The girls decided what we talked about. The guys seemed to be satisfied with the presence of femininity, accepting our reduced input as long as we could admire breasts and curves. The conversation wasn't interesting, only gossip and bragging and jokes, idle nonsense, but everyone put on a show of trying to be interesting. They discussed part-time jobs as if they were careers, reminisced on wild parties and social outings, roasted each other for embarrassing exes.

I wasn't having a bad time, all things considered. There were too many people and I was too mild mannered to get a word in edgewise. Listening was pleasant, if not exactly rewarding.

A girl standing nearby complained that her feet hurt. I told her she could take my chair.

"Oh… a man giving up his seat for a lady. Thanks."

"Sure…?" I said. I looked to see if anyone else found this weird (they hadn't noticed), and scooted down to the grass, nabbing the two beers I had left in the process.

I found myself next to Jules. She had this kind of Annie Hall situation going on, a light gray blouse and open black vest with a blue bow-tie and black jeans, a vintage look I later learned was pieced together from thrift store scrounging. She had bangs hanging over her eyes, which caused her to blow them away with a puff of air every few minutes. Next Monday, I noticed she started wearing her bangs to the side.

"Don't mind her," she said, low and near. "She read some radical feminist essay the other day and now she gets offended whenever a guy does anything polite for her."

"Oh," I said, nodding. "So giving up my seat wasn't chauvinism?"

"Nah. I'm down with eliminating like a trillion sexist social standards, but the whole gentlemanly thing works in our favor, so we should pretty much keep that going forever. You know, as long as you don't expect a reward or anything."

"Oh, for sure. More power to you."

"Hell yeah, man," she said. She leaned back, put her hands on the grass for support, and eyed the two beer bottles between us. "Wanna keep up with the chivalry and offer me one of those?"

"You mean to tell me you actually like beer."

"I'm open to trying to like beer."

"Well alright." I withdrew a bottle opener from my pocket—a metal card-key shaped contraption thin enough to fit in a wallet—and popped the cap off one of the bottles. I handed it to Jules and she knocked it back. She punctuated the action with a refreshed "Ah."

"Okay," she said, "okay. I can get down with this."

We talked. I can't remember what about.

The smoke from the fire started to wade in our direction, stung my eyes and made it hard to breathe. We stood up and, with no place else to stand while still keeping warm, headed for the outside perimeter of the gathering. Just stood there. Neither of us wanted to stay, I don't think. We seemed to be making our way away from the rest of them.

"What's that…?" Jules said, squinting at something between the houses.

I checked out where she was looking. There was definitely something there. A bipedal figure. Not a teenager.

"It's going to be a cop, it's going to be a freakin' cop," she said.

Before I could react, she pulled at my shirt and dashed to the next door neighbor's fence. She climbed over it. I scurried up behind her and plopped to the ground at her side. We crouched. We waited, hoped nobody saw us, hoped no dog currently inhabited this yard.

It took a couple minutes. Eventually the cop made himself known.

"Alright kids! Party's over."

We took turns looking through a hole in the fence. More cops showed up, flashlights shining, blocking all routes of escape except ours. We watched as the kids groaned, forced to dump their beers. The cops didn't notice the water bottles, I was surprised to find. They breathalyzed our friends and wrote tickets. Most of them were under eighteen, so the cops made them call their parents. We listened in on many awkward conversations. About ten minutes later Jules said, "I think it's safe to split now."

We snuck across the yard, climbed over the fence, cut through a few more yards and went out on the sidewalk. We figured we were at a safe enough distance now. No, officer, I had no idea there was underage drinking going on a block away. How irresponsible! No, not something we would do. We're walking home after a shift volunteering at the local soup kitchen.

"Wait, is your car back there?" she asked.

"No, somebody picked me up," I said.

"Same. Fuck. Do you live nearby?"

"Not even close."

We compared how far away our houses were. Hers was closer by a hair.

"Alright. Hey, what the hell. Do you feel like coming over?" she asked.

"Yeah. If you don't mind."

"Yeah, man. You're fun. That was kind of a bummer

party anyway. Kind of an awkward group." We started walking. "So, you ever smoke pot before?" she asked.

"Nope. Never had the opportunity."

"Well, after tonight, you can't say that."

It took us a good half hour to reach her place. We had a pleasant conversation in the meantime. She seemed to have no trouble at all talking to a new person. Most people aren't so open. They put up a shell, leading to shallow discussions rutted with long pauses. Jules had little reservation talking about herself. And she liked asking me questions. Something about her, something inherent she didn't even realize she was doing, made her an inordinately positive presence. She could hyperfocus on making a connection and succeed with no difficulty. I don't know what it was. She was just as messed up and flawed as the next human being. She just managed to make things nice. Didn't contort the ether with insecurities. "Be frank and cordial" would be her motto if she were the type to have a motto.

She talked in depth about her little brother Joshua, who was going to be a sophomore next year. The two were as close as could be. She frowned when I told her I was an only child, like I was missing out on something special.

She liked to cook and grew ecstatic when I explained to her my grandfather's reputation in that field. He was a mildly successful celebrity chef in his day, essentially the seed from which my family's wealth and success had grown. The open secret though, is that my grandmother had been the one with the real skill. She just lacked her husband's gravitas, marketability, and gender privileges. The story impressed Jules and she wanted to know more about them, but—and I enjoy this about her—she didn't come off as jealous of my background.

Her mother, the big moneymaker in the family, worked as a surgeon in a nearby hospital.

"She's a great doctor and all, and even a pretty decent mother, but she's just always busy. We basically grew up with nannies."

"Where's your dad?" I asked.

She shrugged.

"He's somewhere." And left it at that.

We reached her house in the dark. I could see one light on in an upstairs window.

"My dear brother is obsessed with 'cyberpunk' right now, whatever that is," Jules explained. "Either he's watching *Blade Runner* special features or reading some fifty-cent pulp book he found in a church sale."

"That sounds more constructive than what we're doing," I said.

"Like hell. To the garage!"

I'm not sure where she kept her stash. Maybe it changed cyclically. She went into the garage through a side door and rummaged through a thousand drawers and shelves before finding what she wanted.

I waited outside, looking around. Her neighborhood was denser than mine. Less ritzy, but nice. Not bogged down by a draconian homeowners association. It was how a neighborhood should be. Small yards overgrown with gardens. No home over two stories. About half of them were ranch-style. Lots of basketball hoops in driveways. Above-ground pools and hot tubs in the backyards. Trampolines. Jungle gyms. Toys on the sidewalk. Good, wholesome stuff.

Jules returned with a bag in her hand.

"Okay," she said. "We're totally covered if we stand way back over here." She guided me to a nook between the house and garage. Seemed secure. The only vantage points you could see us from were faraway windows.

Jules had me shine my cellphone on her. She took out her product and paraphernalia. There was only a tiny nugget of weed left in the plastic baggie, but she packed it all into the bowl. She pulled out a lighter and demonstrated how to smoke.

"Plug up the hole, let it burn, suck it up, unplug, hold it in, hold it, hooooold it… and let it out."

She followed her own instructions, tilted her head back, mouth to the sky, and guided the smoke in a stream into the air.

"Your turn," she said, handing me the pipe and lighter.

Somehow, I'd never had to handle a normal Bic lighter before. She helped me. Eventually I managed to emulate her actions. It worked out, up until the sucking in. The force and surprise of the burning sensation rushing down my throat was too much and I hacked up a storm. I tried to hold it back, but Jules scolded me.

"Just let it happen," she said. "You're putting weird hippie shit into a body rigidly formed by boring Midwestern suburban principles. Of course it's gonna disapprove at first."

After I recovered, we went in for round two. I got used to it, found humor in it, began to feel light. Like I was floating. The sensation was scarier than I'd imagined. It didn't bring the blissful lethargy it was so renowned for. Maybe later though?

I kept trying to keep pace with Jules. When we finished, only black ashy residue was left inside the concave glass. I felt dizzy. Still float-y. I couldn't focus on a single thought or feeling for too long. This proved problematic. Annoying, even. I thought it was supposed to be impossible to find things annoying when you were high. Wasn't the whole point to be relaxing? What was this?

She took me inside, went to the kitchen, and had me gulp down a tall glass of water. I'd never been so refreshed. I pictured myself after hiking for hours in the heat of the summery Rockies, parched to the point of dehydration, discovering a gorgeous clear spring. The water trickled down smooth gray rocks from an unknown source. The cool liquid felt like it was healing scars in my throat. I tried explaining the sensation to Jules, who looked at me dumbfounded, her expression a workable stand-in for the statement "You are an idiot."

She guided me to her room, which turned out to be surprisingly bare. The decor reminded me of a boarding school dorm or something. Brown furniture and white walls. No posters. Some large framed photos of her friends and family hung around. The stereo looked old and impressive. A couple stuffed animals—Scooby-Doo and a Coca-Cola polar bear—on the modest bed. A desk with a laptop. A few papers sprawled about. Four shelves: One with books, one with CDs, one with more framed photos, and one with what I assumed were notebooks and diaries. Clothes lay in a hamper by the door. Her closet was closed.

I'd expected something completely different. But I guess it wasn't so surprising. There's no way Jules spent much time here. It must have just sufficed for sleeping.

"I'm in the middle of redecorating," she explained, as if reading my thoughts. "I never really changed it since middle school and let it go little girl cute for too long, and now I don't know what the makeover should look like."

Jules pressed some buttons on the stereo and lay down on the bed. She took Scooby-Doo and held him to her chest. I went to the polar bear's side. The music started playing. Acoustic guitar. Moody, whispery singing. We lay side-by-side and stared at the ceiling. Listened.

I felt like I was melting into the bed. It wasn't a good feeling. Scary, actually. And I was having trouble breathing, or remembering to breathe. I wanted to sleep but was too nervous to try. I was worried about her mother popping in. I assumed a boy in Jules' bed wouldn't go down well. But I didn't think about pulling any moves anyway. Jules didn't occur to me as a sexual being right then. Everything was cerebral. Like we were planets, heavenly bodies. And our orbits all of a sudden aligned. And we were just drifting together. Lost. Quiet. Tender and pretty. I don't know. Words like that came to me and lingered. They didn't necessarily mean anything but they felt profound. I was certainly high.

"It was nice to meet you, by the way," Jules said. I pictured her vocal cords. They purred.

"Yeah," I said, the words seeping into the cosmos, aimed nowhere directly. "You too." But it sounded too artificial. I revised: "You definitely too."

She snickered.

" '*You definitely too*,' he says."

We stayed there a long time. I was too nervous to say anything. I kept waiting for Jules to speak up, but she didn't. It became something like boring. Just watching the undulating darkness above me. I started to feel like I had the opportunity to make this beautiful, genuine connection with someone and I was blowing it.

Then I started to think about connections made beyond words. I had this urge to lean toward Jules to find out what she smelled like. It felt like I should have found this out already. Being around her, in her house, in her room.

I fell asleep soon thereafter.

Hours later, probably, Jules rustled me awake and told me she'd drive me home. We stepped outside. The sun was rising. The grass was slick with dew. I liked the smell of wet grass, of a new day. I pulled down the window while Jules was driving and rested my head against the base of the opening, letting the wind take me. I wanted to say it felt like a rebirth, but that was only the cannabis talking. It was noticeably fading, but nowhere near gone.

I wanted to sleep some more.

I hazily directed Jules toward my house. She drove slow, took no road with a speed limit over forty miles an hour. Soon, she pulled into my driveway. I looked at her and realized I didn't want to leave just yet.

"You have a good time?" she asked.

I nodded, still too weak to talk much.

She yawned.

"Catch up with you later then."

I nodded again.

I sat there a little while longer. Nothing more to do. I wanted more to do. But I opened the door and stumbled out instead.

Jules drove away before I got inside the house. I went into my room, looked at my bed, never saw a more comfortable bed in my life, collapsed on it, and slept on my chest till noon. When I woke up, my neck was killing me.

Jules didn't go out of her way to see me after the bonfire at all. Not for any reason, beyond her propensity for finding new and different ways to pass through as many situations and lives as possible.

The connection resumed about a month later though, when we ran into each other at a block party downtown. One of those beginning of summer bonanzas; the kind of event characteristic of my town; the last vestiges of its charming near-rural local eccentricities as it felt the slow encroachment of suburbia.

I'd been walking around with Gabriel, enjoying an uncharacteristically mellow evening in his company, when he left to pursue a sophomore from another school. The kid had recently come out of the closet.

Alone in a crowd, facing the crashing resonant noises and pudgy middle-aged Midwestern bodies and plastic cups of yellow foamy beer, I took refuge by a 7-11, bought an iced coffee and sipped it on a bench, wondering if it might as well be time to head home. Then Jules spotted me. She too had been abandoned by friends looking for potential action (because what else was there to do?), and was all too happy to run into me.

We started talking and found ourselves walking around nearby neighborhoods, listening to the distant muffled noise of unsuccessful-if-semi-listenable local rock bands. We found someone's lawn to sit down and watch the stars on. We shared memes, recommended music to each other. Nothing particularly meaningful developed between us that night. It merely renewed—or maybe reminded her of—her interest in me, and in turn, my fascination with her steadily grew.

Of course, I knew I'd been interested in her ever since the bonfire. I could have done something about it that night. We'd been alone together for such a long time. But I didn't, a conscious choice which I've been turning over in my head ever since.

For a long time, I justified myself by thinking that if I verbalized the way I felt, she would all of a sudden become an intimidating presence to me; someone who I wanted in a specific way and who had the potential to wound me if she didn't want me in that way too.

The more I thought about it though, the more I saw that it wasn't necessary to admit my feelings. Like, I reasoned that it wasn't necessarily love I felt for her. It was my wanting us to keep having this connection, for it to intensify, become more solid. And I wasn't sure how that might happen except to let things be. Like if it were possible for the idea of "us" to bloom into something more, then it must happen of its own accord. One might refer to my inaction as irritatingly passive or, to quote a certain friend of mine, "being a pussy-ass bitch," but I stand by my reasoning. We started to hang out more often after that night, in any case. She enjoyed my companionship; liked just walking around with me, being chill.

"Most people wanna go someplace or have some reason or goal in mind for being out and around," she said. "I just wanna wander."

From there, Jules and I would meet every few weeks. Always spontaneously, us meeting up at some larger event, then splitting off on our own. I got her number at some point, but it didn't matter. She almost never responded to my texts.

I would find her, for instance, at a thrift store, and we'd spend hours finding things for each other, trying things out and judging outfits, then go out to lunch later. I would, and I'm not proud of this part, agree to a movie date with someone, and we'd see Jules there with her friends, and we'd join up, and then, somehow, my date would lose interest, find other friends, and Jules and I would find ourselves on our own, smoking a joint (or rather, her smoking and me politely taking one or two hits) by the dumpsters behind the theater, laughing about whatever generic movie we had just seen. Or, usually, I would see her at a party or a bonfire, and we would drift off on our own, sometimes wind up at my place and play pool in the basement. Swipe drinks discreetly from the liquor cabinet while my dad and his girlfriend watched a movie upstairs.

Though she never went out of her way to plan seeing me, she always seemed to be in my orbit. Accessible only under certain conditions. And I could never ask her about it directly, because it felt too good to hang out with her to put her on the spot like that. The best I could manage was sarcastic comments about how bad she is at texting. To which she'd laugh and go "Yeaaaah I don't know what to tell you, I am literally incapable of change with that sort of thing."

And yet, she checked her phone constantly. As I write this, I look back on that night on the roof, and remember how much time she spent in the blue glow of her iPhone screen, messaging back and forth with Dennis. She never said she was bad with texting specifically. Likely more she meant making plans. Or it could have been that she only texted like that, gave her attention in that way, when she knew someone was in trouble, and her friends were often in trouble, whereas I was just needy and invigorated by her attention.

I'm still not sure if I'm in love with Jules. After all this time, it's odd for me to admit, but it's true. I'm not sure the feeling can be described that way. I mean, it's not lust. Don't get me wrong, I like the way she looks and carries herself, love her style, and it's not like I'd say no if she offered, but she's no more beautiful than I find any number of other people. And it's not quite want or desire in the way those words typically apply to being in love. It feels more like she created a void in my life and then filled it. That's as best as it can be described. She showed me a way of being with another person that I haven't had before or since. If someone else made me feel that way, maybe I could move on from obsessing over her.

To be fair to myself, I am moving on. Slowly, and only just starting now. Not back then though. Then, I was dedicated to going back.

In the fall, before Dennis, Jules told me in snippets how draining last summer had been for her. Her friends had let all their greatest dramas explode within the same small time frame. One confessed that her boyfriend had hit her on multiple occasions—"She says she's dedicated to changing him, but… ugh, don't you just hate it when they think they can unprick a prick? Dating a douchebag I can almost understand, as long as he's occasionally redeeming and not a deadbeat, but dating a douchebag who beats you is beyond me."

Two more friends were arrested for shoplifting and for being drunk and disorderly, not at the same time but within the same week. It was their first time being caught for these offenses, but far from the first time they did them—"They're crazy for sure and that's kinda why I love them, but they've been so much stupider lately."

Then another friend stopped eating because her poor grades prevented her from going to the school she wanted—"She's a smart girl, honestly, but she could just never get it through her skull that grades actually kinda matter. I don't know what to do about her either…"

We talked about these people. Or rather, she talked and I listened. My advice was of that obvious lukewarm variety, offered in marginal spurts wedged between her rounds of venting.

Manic pixie dream girl. The romantic comedy trope. The amazingly quirky super-hot misfit who magically solves the disillusioned male protagonist's problems by guiding him through hard times, as if it were her only obligation, creating a false standard for dudes who willingly describe themselves as "hopelessly romantic," deluding themselves into believing there's a girl out there whose one joy is to serve them.

Does anyone still talk about this or are we too irony poisoned to take it seriously as a criticism of art? Is it a bit gauche to talk about? I don't know. All I know is

that as overplayed as the trope is, and as much as me-
dia-addled people on the internet roll their eyes when
you bring it up, it feels relevant.

Boys, maybe me—maybe especially me—wanted
Jules to be that girl. She didn't get asked out a lot, but
if there were a contest for Most Crushed Upon in our
high school, Jules would have placed highly. We talked
about this when my friendship with Jules gained public
attention. For a while, guys approached me in this anxious onset of jealousy and asked if we were dating, and
if so, what I'd done to be so lucky. I humbly denied the
assumption, though rumors persisted.

I mentioned it to her one day, hoping it insinuated
something to her. She just groaned.

"Ugh. Don't you hate when people see a guy and a
girl together and they just assume? It's such a pain being friends with guys. And guys can't be friends with too
many girls or they'll be called gay or whatever. Gender
sucks. We should get rid of it."

"Putting that in your campaign speech?"

"Right after free medical marijuana for every Amer-
ican."

"Economically questionable, but alright."

"Yep. At least my friends never thought we were together. They think you're gay actually, I'm pretty sure."

"I was getting that vibe. Is it the shoes or what?"

"You're not an athlete, you're not in a band, you have
fashion sense. And, like, not that it bothers me, but you
did famously make out with a guy at a party once. Gay
through and through for most people."

"Huh. I don't know. It's probably the shoes."

"You're also an old man."

"Am I really?"

"You watch black-and-white Japanese movies while sipping sherry. You listen to history podcasts while practicing pool shots in your basement. Don't give me that."

She never questioned my bisexuality. It was as if she knew from the start and just rolled with it. She never treated me like a gay best friend, the way some girls tried to with me. Never reduced me to a curiosity, a sidekick.

In fact, she wasn't really threatened by my being attracted to her at all.

I remember one night, when we were playing pool, I managed to sink the eight-ball despite her last ball being right in the path. It was a tense game, and we'd been going back and forth for about half an hour, so in the exasperation of finally losing, she jumped on my back and tackled me to the carpet.

"You absolute bastard!" she yelled. "The game's rigged! Balls are weighted! Table's crooked! The whole system's corrupt!"

I fought back gently, not really wanting her to get off of me. She didn't get close to me too often. Usually, it was a casual pat on the back in a moment of camaraderie, or pushing me after a particularly bad joke.

In the rush of the moment and feeling her against me I got a... well, she noticed something. And to her immense credit instead of awkwardly withdrawing and never speaking about it, letting me stew in the embarrassment for eternity, she stopped, looked me right in the eye and said, "Glad to know I've still got it," and then burst out laughing. We ended up next to each other sitting against the wall, still on the floor, till the giggles passed.

"Seriously, man," she said, "don't feel bad. It happens."

Her acknowledging it made me more embarrassed. I must have turned beet red, because she laughed even more.

And then, somehow, Jules directed the conversation so that we started talking about people that we liked at school. I don't know how I was able to talk about it without mentioning her. One of those elephants in the room that is so large, addressing it feels redundant, maybe.

Jules only mentioned guys. She didn't seem to have a type. She rattled off a list of guys she'd been interested in, who'd asked her out, who she'd even made out with once or twice. I'm sure she was hooking up with guys beyond that at the time, and perhaps intuiting my discomfort with picturing it, she didn't delve into those details. But what she did do was tell embarrassing stories about herself. Like when a guy broke up with her sophomore year by writing a letter and sending it with a cake that had the words "SORRY BABE" written over her picture in printed fondant on top. And he happened to send it when she was having a sleepover at her house, meaning all her friends learned about it and spread the story immediately.

"That feels more embarrassing for him than you," I pointed out.

"Well, I haven't mentioned the part where I ate the whole thing in the corner that night with my bare hands while crying in front of my friends."

"You ate his break-up cake?"

"What else am I supposed to do with it, huh? It's my break-up cake."

"Good point. Well, was it at least any good?"

"Nah. Too dry and too much sugar in the icing. I gotta make sure my next boyfriend is a better baker."

We laughed some more, and the conversation drifted back to attractive people.

"That buddy of yours Gabriel isn't too shabby," she observed. "Though of course I'm kind of out of the game there."

"Yeah," I said. "I've tried starting something with him before, actually. But he doesn't really go for guys who aren't younger than him."

"Cradle-robber, huh?" she commented. She didn't even bat an eye at my admission. "Weird. So he like turned you down or…?"

"Nah, we just tend to hook up here and there, then go back to being friends. We're too set in our dynamic now to do anything else, I think."

"That's kind of sad, don't you think? I mean, I don't think there's a single man-on-man couple in our whole school for us girls to fetishize."

"Oh we would be a terrible couple though. No question."

"Ah well, if you say so."

She offered to try and set me up with guys or girls she knew, and I said I wasn't looking for anything right now.

"I'd offer you the same," I said. "But it feels like you don't have any issues with that."

She shrugged.

"Believe it or not, it's tough for me too, thank you

very much. But I'm with you, I'm not looking for anything right now. Too much other stuff to deal with. Not enough time in the day to bother with a boyfriend."

That was where our relationship conversations always ended. She would say she either didn't have the energy to commit to a boyfriend, or didn't have the fortitude to commit to one boyfriend, or something else like that. And she'd mention polyamory half-seriously, and we would joke about her being the epicenter of some great eldritch multi-partner relationship whose mighty tendrils threaten to take over the entire Midwest and eventually the whole world.

Like I've said before, I don't know exactly what I wanted with Jules. I only knew I wanted how I felt in those times we shared together back. I really should have known, from the moment she left the rooftop that night, that we couldn't go back.

"I'm tired," she said once.

"How so?" I asked.

"School, friends… I don't know. I feel really irrelevant here."

"Irrelevant is okay. Boring is what you watch out for."

"Sure. No, I mean, I'm fine, obviously. I'm always going to be fine. I just wish… ugh. I don't know. I just wish I felt more like myself, y'know?"

"There's certainly nobody who can claim to be you, Jules."

"Yeah, yeah. Maybe it's just hormones or whatever. I'm just so not content with myself."

"Stressed?"

"Constantly. But that's fine, that's ordinary."

"What do you want then?"

"Huh?"

"Like, what do you think would make this thing that's bothering you stop bothering you?"

"Oh. A change of scenery, maybe."

"The Midwest getting you down?"

"It's okay here. But I'd like to know how it is somewhere else."

6 – Something I have to do for myself

The optimistic acceptance of my luck in life—that all the people in this world haven't had the advantages I've had, as Nick Carraway had taught me—dulled over the winter. I continued to spend too much time frivolously preoccupied with matters beyond my control, plagued by the abstract sadness I thought I'd killed back in Madison.

I was more and more aware of my isolation, my place in that prison with golden bars. Despite a good reputation at school, nobody really called me their friend. The last person who had really desired a connection with me was Gabriel, and I hadn't hung out with him in months. My old friends no longer concerned themselves with me. Estelle said hi sometimes, but indicated no interest beyond that. I was at that stage where everybody keeps themselves at a safe and superficial distance, allowing me to wallow alone in this guise of detached superiority.

I worked and read and drank and thought about a girl. I missed Jules. It had to be faced. Thinking about her didn't help. It made matters worse. The ghost left by her absence still loomed overhead. So unnecessary, it seemed. This girl who I only ever knew in tiny unreliable glimpses of intimacy. I wanted to know how she was doing, if she would ever come back, if she thought about me every once in a while, if she would even want to see me again.

I bumped up my hours working at the bars and restaurants, so nearly all my time was occupied by school, homework, F. Scott Fitzgerald novels, and work. A month and a half passed on this busy schedule. Midwestern weather teased spring with days of surprising warmth, only to regress back into the icy bite of winter.

On those warm nights, Gordon and I would sit on the roof and smoke cigars. He would tell stories of his youth, usually concerning vandalism (for art and activism, of course), recreational drug use, short-cutting his way through academics, and chasing after women with something close to a fervency. Gordon talked in circles and circles, enthusiastic and distracting. He was so far out and muddled that he no longer needed conversation, just a wall to bounce his voice off of. I didn't mind. There was wisdom somewhere within all that hot air.

Cigars were a new experience. I received no satisfaction from them, no relaxing buzz, but according to Gordon, they were damn fine cigars, so I kept experimenting. It's one of my missions to appreciate all quality things as much as possible, whether or not they're pleasurable in my subjective experience, and cigars had been on the list for a while.

Gordon told me one story about how he and a friend walked five miles to a diner because they were high and had no car. The friend found a brochure that promised amazing coffee and rhubarb pie. While enjoying their amazing coffee and rhubarb pie, a couple drunken bikers got into a brawl in front of them, threatening each other with steak knives. Gordon and his friend, confident or stupid, rushed in and broke it up, eventually kicking the bikers out. Subsequently, they hit it off with the manager, who secured jobs for them at the diner for the next six months, until they were fired for selling weed on the clock. In the manager's defense, Gordon added, he was more mad at them for selling on company time than for the selling itself.

"It's funny," he said. "When you're running at full throttle for so long, it doesn't occur to you to look back. Now that I can… damn, how in the hell am I not dead in a ditch a dozen times over? Can't say I have many regrets though. No sir. Gotta be impulsive, kid. Best decisions you'll ever make are the ones you don't think about."

When we had talked over New Year's Eve, Estelle had mentioned playing guitar at a local cafe every now and then.

I checked out the cafe, found out when they were playing next, and went to the performance. I sat at a table by a window apart from the crowd.

Estelle did acoustic covers of popular artists, extrapolating on the otherwise simple chorus-heavy music. Their voice had a crisp edge to it, a bite lingering in familiar bluesy silkiness. And strumming came smooth and easy from their fingers.

I sat drinking the cafe's signature medium roast coffee, which tasted like burnt caramel popcorn, and kept hoping my tongue would eventually acquire the taste. It took half the mug for me to realize the coffee was just bad.

Estelle was midway through a rendering of Years & Years' "King." They had good stage presence. Attractive, secure, really in the moment. The cafe patrons went about chatting, laughing, clinking on porcelain or glass, chewing crispy fries and chips and sandwiches with hard, loud bread. Estelle's lovely tunes entered into the cacophony smoothly, without complaint.

The audience applauded lightly when they finished their set. They put their things away and climbed off stage. Easy listening jazz started playing through the speakers to make up for the sudden drop in noise. Over at a high table, a friend waited for them with two drinks already ordered. I recognized her as a girl named Lana who I'd had class with a few times.

Estelle didn't notice me. I didn't expect them to. I successfully melded into the scenery, another average Joe hanging out.

Insofar as any such call can be made by an outside observer, Estelle looked more like themself lately. More comfortable inhabiting their own body in public space, maybe. Not that their style changed enormously, but their sense of fashion, which was typically a straight-forward femme look with little queer identifiers, like earrings with the non-binary pride flag colors, now had a much more pronounced soft butch vibe. I always seemed to see them in either a red leather or torn-up jean jacket. They cut their hair short, a pixie style with a zigzag pattern in the fade, got a little cut in their left eyebrow.

Not enormous changes when it came down to it, but small, significant ones.

My impulse was to go up to Lana and Estelle, despite mental blocks popping up like "What if I interrupt some personal conversation?" or "What if we have nothing to say to each other and I just make things awkward?" But Gordon's no-thinking-needed policy was still fresh in my mind, so I went over to them.

I said hello and complimented Estelle's music, asked to sit with them.

The following hour or so worked out well. We had a conversation. Words exchanged between us in an agreeable way. We said funny things and laughed. We talked about Estelle's musical preferences, the dichotomy between what they liked to listen to and what they liked to play. We talked about school, things we hated about it and things we thought we might soon miss. I listened to their post-grad plans—Lana to the University of Illinois at Urbana-Champaign, Estelle to a tiny liberal arts college not too far from home. They got into an argument about environmental policy and organic food. They got into an argument about whether it's morally reprehensible to continue to listen to Chris Brown or Drake while calling yourself a Rihanna fan.

"I just think you have to separate the art from the artist," Lana said. "That's all."

Estelle gave Lana a look like they were about to vomit at the very notion.

"Well it's not like I'm going to their concerts or anything!" Lana said. "But if I'm in the mood for 'Furthest Thing,' I'm in the mood for 'Furthest Thing.' That's all. Why are you looking at me like that?"

"Girl, I…" Estelle began. Then they seemed to think better of it. "No, it's fine. You're not the problem but… Listen, Chris Brown freaks me out in, like, an ordinary boring masc ain't shit kind of way, and I can't ever justify supporting him. But Drake is *creepy*. He is *insidious*."

"Sure. And if I want to get in my feelings, I'm listening to 'Furthest Thing.' I don't know what to tell you."

Estelle laughed at that and didn't follow up.

I interjected that I still watched Roman Polanski movies sometimes and felt bad about it. They both gave me a look, not like they didn't know who I was talking about but more like, why was I interrupting their banter.

"Wait, didn't he do the one where Johnny Depp opens a portal to hell?" Lana said.

"Yeah," I said.

"That's a good one."

Estelle shook their head.

"Haven't seen it, but wow, Johnny Depp too? Next you'll tell me the hair and make-up lady was a war criminal."

Then, as if in penance for even invoking the name of Chris Brown, they turned their conversation to when Rihanna would release a new album. Any minute now, they agreed.

Soon, Lana said she had to go, and Estelle took off a few minutes later. We exchanged numbers.

That night, they texted me saying it was fun chatting. I told them the same. Casually, we made plans to meet up at my place over the weekend.

I did not expect to have sex with Estelle that night. It had not even crossed my mind that Estelle considered me a potential partner. But it happened. No precedent of getting comfortable, no preliminary getting-to-know-you phase. They wanted sex, and knew I was able to offer it to them. No shame or tiptoeing

It started out innocently enough. They came over to my house. I showed them around. We talked about friends and family. Then I mentioned that my father

91

would be gone for the weekend. That seemed to trigger something.

"Oh," they said. You could almost see the light bulb over their head. "Cool. Wanna show me your room?"

I should have known the agenda from this moment on. It was unexpected though. Sex didn't register as a possibility, so the insinuation didn't process for me. It all clicked though when I brought them to my room and they took me to the bed.

"Oh!" I said, taken aback when they started kissing me. "We really doing this?"

"You don't want to?"

"No I do, it's just a little fast."

"I'll walk you through it," they said, cupping the back of my head and pulling me in. "Come on."

I wasn't *un*confident in what to do, even if I'd never really gotten this far with someone before. No fear, not really. Ordinary levels of nervousness. A slight confusion, a feeling that we should have talked more before this whole situation started. Loss of control, maybe.

Between kisses, they took off their red leather jacket, took off my shirt. We kissed some more. My hands went to unbutton and unzip their black jeans. They took my hands and placed them aside, then removed the jeans themself. I'd go to remove something and they'd stop me and take off the article themself. This rhythm went on until we were naked. Nothing was too terribly wrong with this—the end result was the same after all—but it was confusing.

Foreplay proved odd. Estelle kissed and touched in a clinical way, clearly wanting to delve deeper under the covers, but doing so without any obvious indication of pleasure, more curious than enthusiastic. Sensing this stoicism, I tried to lighten the mood, giggling between kisses, cracking dumb jokes. Other than rolling their eyes at the really bad ones, they didn't give me much anything in return.

For Christmas last year, Jonathan half-mockingly gave me a cookie jar filled with condoms. It was on my desk. Now I hopped up to get one.

"Easy, okay?" they said, with the passion of a flight attendant's safety instructions. "Go slow."

I either did or thought I did. We didn't get into it for very long though. I got the impression they were only experimenting, examining the sensations, and my anxiety over this did not do any favors toward my own enjoyment. It soon became boring and uncomfortable.

I didn't get off and neither did they. They just stopped after a certain point and went to the bathroom.

We didn't talk much afterwards. Funny to think such a rift could form between me and somebody I'd just been inside of.

When they came back out, they walked to the pile of our clothes next to the bed and started to redress.

"You alright?" they asked, not interrupting their process, not looking at me.

"Um, yeah," I said, naked in bed, half covered by sheets. "Fine. You?"

"Good," they replied, nodding. "Yeah, good. Sorry, I had to stop. Something was up with my stomach."

I didn't quite believe that, given how they delivered the line like an excuse, but was glad they had stopped once they decided they weren't comfortable with the situation.

"Okay, no problem."

It wasn't late, but I felt exceedingly tired. I thought about asking questions like "So… what does this make us?" or "Is this a one time thing, or…?" or "Do you do this often or was it just me?" The words wouldn't form though. The gods who prevent clingy dudes from using clichés intervened. Silence spread instead.

"I have to go home now," they said, slipping on their jacket, "but I'll hit you up later, 'kay?" They leaned down and kissed me. "Bye for now."

This "for now" was apparently indefinite.

They made no attempt to contact me after that, no longer even gave their little hellos when we crossed paths in school.

I fought the urge to reach out to them myself, convinced they now had no interest in me.

It was funny, looking at the points where our lives had intersected. They had stalked me, I had bullied them, we had ignored each other, we had forgotten each other, we had remembered each other one New Year's Eve in Madison, we had kissed while watching *Friends*, we had talked in a cafe, we'd had an abrupt and sub-par sexual encounter… and finally they had gone back to ignoring me.

Maybe the whole thing was a sort of conquest for them. Long game domination of an old bully. Or maybe they thought I was someone they could like, and all of a sudden, their feelings had changed. That has been known to happen.

Could have been a million things. I pushed the incident away. It was now just another thing that had happened to me. I was no longer a pure, undefiled youth and I felt no different. Estelle could have played a larger part in my life, but they didn't.

Winter fell away with no strong emotions in any direction. I brought my hours at the bars and restaurants down to the usual amount. I ran a lot, read a lot of books, re-read *The Great Gatsby* twice, thinking more and more about Nick Carraway. I bought a bunch of different kinds of high-end tea and tasted them together. Then, bored with this, sampled them with the high-end whiskeys and brandy in our liquor cabinet. I cooked and watched movies with my father.

My emotions weren't getting better, but they weren't getting worse. I thought maybe I was privileged to a life of lonely contentment, if not exactly happiness.

Closing time at Hyde's Place one night, I was tossing trash into the dumpster behind the bar when I heard somebody yell my name. I saw a figure through the alleyway. He ran toward me. I waited for him to approach, wondering why he was running so fast, and before I knew it, he had knocked me to the ground and pressed his knee into my chest.

One hand went around my neck, another clenched into a fist and struck me, hard and without form. As he raised it for another blow, I peeled his hand off my neck and tried throwing him off. The motion seemed clumsy and weak, but it worked.

I jumped to my feet at the moment of release and backed away from the attacker.

The rush of aggression drained out of both of us.

He was on his hands and knees, looking up at me.

"You..." he whimpered. He took a deep breath in, then exhaled loudly. He got to his feet. The rabid assailant shriveled into a quivering man-child. His lower lip stuck out, trembling. His eyes were wide and glistening, ready to burst into tears.

I recognized this guy from school. A kid in my grade named Max. Never been in a class with him. Never once directed a thought at him. Just another student, another face.

"Hi," he said in a mockery of politeness, with a smile that tried to disguise how upset he was. "So I heard that you slept with my ex-girlfriend."

My face stung. Would probably have a bruise later. I thought about being furious at Max, then thought better of it. He wasn't the same creature he'd been a moment ago. Now he was rage subsided, shell cracked, the yolk left on the ground.

I brought him inside. Gordon and a younger bartender were the only ones left, and they were about done with the clean-up.

"Damn, we missed the fight club again!" Gordon chided, belting out an exaggerated laugh. I'm not sure how he took everything in stride like that. No follow-up questions, nothing.

"Shit, you guys okay?" the younger bartender said, more in touch with what basic human responses look like.

"We're good," I said. "Just a scuffle."

96

I promised Gordon I'd close up and, since he asked, hire only a few prostitutes. They left within the next ten minutes.

Max sat in a booth trembling, mumbling, feeling bad for himself. He didn't look capable of violence anymore. He looked more like one of those mental patients in a B-movie who just rocks back and forth for hours, having seen some horror beyond their understanding. It felt exaggerated. Nothing so horrific could have happened to a guy like Max. He was blowing it out of proportion, I knew. Someone he liked did something he didn't want them to. And by the sound of it, someone he liked had also accepted an identity he didn't want them to accept, or one he didn't understand.

I made two gin and tonics and put on some Miles Davis, trying to flip this harsh red atmosphere into something cool and blue. I sat down across from him and set the drinks on coasters. Max didn't touch it, didn't even acknowledge it there in front of him.

"Okay," he said, staring at the edge of the table. "I am going to tell you a story. And you are not going to say another word until I finish. Okay?"

I nodded. He must have seen it out of his peripherals, because then he began.

"Alright. We didn't date for that long, I admit," he said. "The fact that I'm still so insane about it is actually a big part of why I'm still so insane about it. But, look, I found out you two had slept together. Heard it from a friend of a friend. Don't ask me how they found out. Everybody finds out everything eventually. Anyway, it upset me. I had to hurt something. It was too much to process."

The glass in front of him started to sweat. A bead trickled down the side and sank into the cardboard coaster. He touched his finger to the side of the glass, wetting it, and drew circles on the table.

"I guess I kept thinking that she wasn't ready for what I wanted," he contemplated.

"They weren't ready, you mean," I corrected.

"Shut up," he said, and glared at me.

I wanted to point out that perhaps getting constantly misgendered might have informed Estelle's decision to dump him, but I didn't say anything. I just threw up my hands as if to say, "Hey, I tried."

A moment later, he resumed his speech.

"I hoped she would come around eventually, and I'd be there waiting with the exact amount of feeling as before. But she was done, wasn't she? Done a long time ago. We dated for like eight seconds, it seems like. But there was something about it... I wanted so bad to be somebody to her. I just can't deal with the fact that one moment, you have the potential to be somebody who she can't live without, and the next you might as well be a stranger. I thought I'd be prepared for that. You expect relationships to end with some big argument or catastrophe. That's not it though.

"I wish it didn't bother me so much. Like, I'm a reasonably happy guy. I have interests. I have a life. I have goals. But everything gets bogged down by useless feelings for this girl. And I can't hate her. It would be so much easier to hate her, but she's too genuinely wonderful to hate. She's got flaws, everybody's got flaws, but not enough to hate her. It's so weird to think somebody else's pursuit of happiness can make you miserable. It's got nothing to do with me, so it shouldn't affect me, right? But it hurts exactly because it's got nothing to do with me.

"Then she sleeps with you. I remember you, you know? I remember what you did. You were a dick to her years ago, and after this extraordinarily long period of silence you up and fuck her. It's too absurd. And yet... I can't hate you either. I'd have done the same thing in your position."

Max broke off, took a sip of gin and tonic. The lime fell between two ice cubes.

"She broke up with me after that kid killed himself, actually," he admitted. "That hit her pretty bad. Didn't know him, but all the same... I think she needed to be alone after that. She realized that life's short and started doing things more for herself. She didn't really give me a reason beyond that for breaking up with me. Just didn't need it. Just wanted to be by herself. 'You don't have to do this all by yourself,' I said. 'Yes I do,' she said. I can't match up to that, man."

He drank more. I drank too. I tried making eye contact again. He didn't return it.

"And here we are. I don't want to hear anything you have to say. I just needed to get that all out. I'm angry. I'm not going to be okay. My priorities are fucked. I'm stuck wishing girls would like me more. Something happened to me and I've been conditioned into this. Fuck, man. I might be successful one day. I might be wealthy. But I'm never going to be happy unless some girl is interested in me. I know how hopeless I'm becoming and I'm allowing myself to be hopeless."

He gulped the rest of his drink and set it down on

the table. He sighed, stood, and walked away. I heard the back door open and close.

Curious and with a bag of frozen peas to my eye, I spent the later hours of the night creeping on Max's social media. A lot of things I had a feeling about clicked into place for me.

He posted several "dark humor" memes that were really just a Trojan horse for racism. The kind suburban white boys think they can pass off as joking around. Stereotypes about Africa, fake gangster lingo, badly appropriating AAVE. That sort of thing. I could hardly judge him, I wasn't really that far away from the days when I, well, never posted these kinds of memes. But I did use to at least like or favorite them.

But okay. Obviously, there was more to Estelle breaking up with him than just being done with him in some abstract sense. Less Estelle saying "I'm just not feeling it anymore" and more them saying, "I have no time for your ignorance anymore."

He interspersed these with rambling posts about being sad and how girls suck. Sometimes, even with an unflattering selfie.

Taking all of what I knew of him, I couldn't avoid comparing myself to Max. The sadsack who grasps to define himself through intimate connections, who then fails and suffers under the shadow of heartbreak, feeling vindictive against the world. I had not yet even experienced a break-up, just consistent failure to get the blood flowing in the first place. But I understood that Max's desires were misguided, striving for someone to fulfill him and for him to in some way do the same for them, even though he had nothing to offer but this false benevolence. The loser nice guy attitude that has fueled teen dramedies for decades.

It clicked for me, despite thinking that I already knew it; that I wanted Jules to be with me for all the wrong reasons. It was an unhealthy expectation, using her companionship to supplement my happiness. My presence did not please her the same way hers pleased me. Jules didn't want other people the way I did. She didn't feel alone the way I did.

There is no excuse for what I did next, except that I was lonely and confused and so I drifted toward the last person who had made me feel less lonely and confused. I visited the coffee shop every time Estelle played. I didn't go up and talk to them, didn't press my presence. It was a different kind of desperation than longing for a romantic partner, though now I realize that it was in effect, the same to Estelle. I just wanted to be in their sight, in some way. Have someone there who knew me, who had a reflection of myself within them, who could acknowledge, however indirectly, that I still existed.

They talked to me, though not much. Thanked me for coming and made short, polite small talk before going off to do something else. Then as I kept going, clearly making them uncomfortable it seemed to me, they stopped doing even that and only waved or said hi in passing. The kinds of gestures you make to someone who you would really prefer stay a memory.

Estelle seemed to have gotten closer to Lana. Lana,

too, was at the coffee shop almost every time Estelle played. The body language between the two was different than before. More casually touching, literal and emotional closeness. I considered what this might have meant.

I happened to read recently an article about gender transition leading to discovering parts of one's sexual identity not before explored, because it didn't make sense under one's former gender role. Maybe I didn't make sense to Estelle as they continued to explore themself. It seemed I had been a stepping-stone, or an experiment, or a loose thread. Something, in any case, that they had to consider before moving on.

Well, I must have been considered.

Another thing though, was that I admired the shit out of Estelle. I'd seen them go from someone I had mistreated and had given absolutely no fucks about, to someone with a level of self-assurance and self-worth I couldn't even attempt to emulate.

I wanted so badly to be like them. To understand them. It felt like a bitter irony, or maybe just deserts, that now they had no interest in me whatsoever.

The last time I visited the coffee shop, which was no great loss for their coffee, by the way, Lana took a seat at my table while Estelle was playing.

"Hey," she said. Polite, but pointed. Here for a reason, no idle chit-chat. I think she was kind about it because she knew me enough in passing to know I wouldn't be toxic. Just perhaps inadvertently invasive.

"Hi," I said.

"Look, my guy," she began. "I'm not going to tell you where to hang out, but I think you and I both know why you keep coming back here."

That was all she needed to say for me to snap out of it. She didn't have to say "You're making Estelle uncomfortable" or "They're just not into you" or anything like that. Because maybe, somehow, Lana knew it wasn't about me wanting Estelle again. Maybe she intuited that it was me clinging to someone I had felt a brief intimacy with, because that was all I had at the time, and I didn't want to let it go, no matter how brittle the connection.

I turned bright red with embarrassment.

"I know," I said. I took one last big gulp of my burnt-flavored coffee. Lana just looked at me, not unkindly, but not friendly either. "Tell them I'm sorry, if you want."

I got up, set the mug in the bin, and went to make my way out of that coffee shop for good. Before I could, Lana caught me by the elbow. I noticed her wrist ringed with colorful hemp bracelets.

"Wait, dude," she said. "Cool it with the dramatics."

I stopped and turned to her, averted my eyes in shame.

"Look, you're clearly going through something here," she continued. "I don't want to make you feel bad. In fact, I'd like to help if I can. Not that I know you super well but just putting it out there: I run a couple queer support groups. I'm not sure where you are on that, but you're welcome to find me online if you're interested."

I nodded, told her thanks.

"I'll think about it," I said.

"Sure," she answered. "Take care, okay?" Then she

went back into the coffee shop. The bells chimed and faded out as the door closed.

I saw Estelle's silhouette from out of the corner of my eye as I turned to head down the street. The part of my brain that thinks in cinematic convention tried to construe this as a bittersweet goodbye, of two people meaningfully parting. Only it wasn't really.

It never stops amazing me how fast people come and go from your life.

7 – Alleyways and parking lots

April. My birth month, the precipice of summer. Nearly three out of four seasons had now gone by since Jules' departure.

My father and I made a hearty shepherd's pie dinner for my eighteenth birthday; accompanied it with dark creamy lagers and bread pudding for dessert. We watched *The Big Sleep* together and afterwards discussed how watching this movie expecting to understand the plot was the wrong attitude. We compared Raymond Chandler to similar writers, wondering if that sort of mystery fiction is outdated in novel form now that we have movies.

Neither of us maintained a strong opinion, instead, we leveled the debate from both sides, going back and forth with observations and agreements. The conversation eventually devolved into rating how hot the most popular actresses of the time were. Lauren Bacall, we both agreed.

My father asked me if I planned on having friends over. I said no. It wasn't necessary. A birthday was just another day to me now. He said he knew what I meant.

"You are getting older," he said.

He went to bed early, right after we finished washing the dishes.

I wanted to watch another movie in which men and women drank and smoked to excess in black-and-white, so I put on *Casablanca*. I drank one drink, then another, then another, and eventually lost count. The movie went in and out of focus, my tired head wandering.

It was a good day though, all things considered. I received a few phone calls from family members wishing me a fantastic day, promising cards and gifts in the mail any day now. My father bought me a new suit. I thanked my family in advance, thanked my father for everything.

Around eleven o'clock that night the doorbell rang. I opened it to the sight of a car speeding down the street. On the doorstep sat a cardboard box, unmarked and duct-taped along the top. I brought it into the kitchen, already vaguely aware of the sender, and cut it open with a steak knife.

A glass bottle of absinthe lay inside. A quality brand judging from the elaborate label. A note was attached by a rubber band around the neck.

It read: "Stolen from a frat party. Don't ever think I'd spend money on you. Happy birthday."

Gabriel and Jules had never met. I wondered if they would have liked each other if they ever had. Gabriel, the only other really extreme influence in my life. His uncontrolled passions led to these fascinatingly volatile and self-destructive behaviors. Manipulative, selfish, yet somehow sweet. There were two Gabriels: The persona he sold and the one he kept to the interior, revealed through cracks intentionally or unintentionally. Like an aggressive pop-punk song with offputtingly sincere romantic lyrics. Things that made him cling to these faux-innocent boys like Tate so dearly.

I knew plenty of guys Gabriel had pursued and plenty he'd gone on a date or two with, but I only met one of Gabriel's serious boyfriends before. He was a confident kid named Dade, in fact, the boy he'd left me to pursue at the block party last summer. They had been dating for about two months at that point. The relationship lasted about the duration of summer. I could only hope he was at least sixteen. The age gap between sixteen and seventeen is somehow a gulf, but it can make sense with the right people. But when a sixteen-year-old is with someone years older, I can't help but feel like the older person is kind of a creep.

We met under a concrete bridge in a secluded park one night. The park covered a good chunk of the floodplain on either side of a river, and was completely submerged almost every year during the rainy season. We shined flashlights on the curved line under the bridge, hung out in the rubble, careful to avoid needles and trash on the ground. Gabriel had brought some spray cans with him and started spray painting a mural of Bill Murray as a Rastafarian. He kept talking about graffiti as the purest art form because it's done neither for fame nor recognition.

"I wish I had big clever messages behind everything I do," he said. "But for now it's all just Bill Murray."

"Didn't know you were into graffiti," I said.

"He's not really," Dade chimed in. "It just started all of a sudden."

Dade, his smooth pale face flushed red in the evening chill, wore a green sweater with large brown buttons. I don't know how Gabe kept finding these androgynous, too-beautiful-for-words Tadzios. I'm sure I would have noticed if one had ever crossed my path. But Gabe had his ways. It was like his near constant, aggressive pursuit somehow manifested them into existence.

These kids always had this curious effect on Gabriel. He was quieter around the objects of his affection, more respectful, more reserved. Like he didn't want to do anything to offend them. I had seen this behavior in passing, if I happened to catch him on a date or in the process of trying to woo someone. He didn't act the way he did with me—rough and blunt.

"Doesn't he scare you a little?" I asked, when Gabriel ran out into the bushes to relieve himself.

"Pft, no. He's a teddy bear," Dade said sharply.

That was the other thing about these boys: They weren't oblivious. They knew exactly how they looked, that sweet and innocent persona emanating from their uniformly gentle expressions, and they knew how to exploit people's reactions to them. They might just destroy you if you underestimated them.

"He's more scared of me."

"I'd love to know your secret," I joked.

"I think we both know what it is," he said, winking at me.

It's weird, I never really had any insecurities about my appearance, but that comment made me feel insecure for the rest of the night. Such a subtle dig. Like, way to make it painfully aware that I am not attractive in the right way to Gabriel, and if I was, he would act completely differently toward me. Not that I wanted to look like Dade, or necessarily wanted Gabriel to act toward me the way he acted toward Dade. But with that comment he made me feel inadequate for not being able to achieve the kinds of responses people offered Dade.

Despite his sharp edges, I found myself enjoying Dade that night. At least I was amused by him. He was nice to look at, for one thing, and he could say things to Gabriel that I could never have gotten away with.

"I'm cold and bored, Gabe," he complained. "Can we go yet?"

"I'll be done soon here," Gabriel said between the sizzle of spray paint, way chiller than he normally would. "Just gotta get his dreads right."

Dade groaned and pouted, tapping his foot impatiently in what looked like an "adorably bratty" routine I bet he practiced in the mirror.

"Hey," Gabriel said, "can we hang out at Hyde's Place after this?"

I didn't feel like hanging out with them all night since I was already feeling like a third wheel, so I made some excuse.

"Hyde's Place?" Dade asked. "The dive bar?"

I explained and Dade grilled me on my background. Once he realized I was the heir to a small culinary empire, he had a much less dismissive attitude toward me. I wonder what he thought of Gabriel then, seeing how little that guy could call his own, how bleak his prospects, given his abusive home situation and his proclivity to fuck around with petty crime, rather than apply himself to anything that might improve his life even marginally. But then, he was with Gabriel and not me. I was the one to be admired from a distance, while Gabriel was the one I saw him on top of in the backseat of Gabriel's car as I started to walk home later that night.

That was the only time I saw him together with Dade. Gabriel never brought Dade again when we hung out the rest of the summer. He would mention him and would presumably hang out with him on the nights he wasn't with me. Then one night in late August I asked how Dade was doing. Gabriel just shook his head and said, "Didn't work out." Left no room for questioning.

My friend Gabriel, who I had grown fond of through moments of excruciating sadness.

It feels like Gabriel and I had known each other from the start. We went to the same elementary school, well before the neighborhoods got so heavily class divided and the upper-crust parents forced a change in school districts. We didn't go to middle school together, but we re-met in high school. He was never impressed with me. Even when I acted like a jackass, he could see right through me.

I don't know why he decided to be my friend when I was still my worst self, but he did.

It was early our junior year at another party. Only, this was one of my rich kid parties. The kind you find deep, deep in the McMansion outskirts of town. Gabriel adored crashing these things, raiding their supply of alcohol and prescription drugs, knowing nobody would want to mess with him.

I sat on a couch in a crowd of preppy stereotypes, sipping on PBR because the richer you are, the worse you drink at parties. I zoned out the way I'd started to at these gatherings, increasingly uninterested in whatever anyone was saying: conversations about graduating early and heading to an Ivy League on a legacy scholarship or whatever.

Gabriel came crashing in. He never slipped onto the scene, he always crashed. Swung the front door open and walked onto the living room carpet with his shoes still on, even though the rest of us were barefoot.

"Sup, assholes?" he said, not even looking at anyone, eyeing the crystalline liquor cabinet in the corner. He grabbed a decanter full of brown liquid, sniffed at it and poured himself a glass.

A chunk of the crowd stopped talking and stared at him.

"What?" he asked after one good swig. "Oh, right, sorry. I forget you pendejos don't see Mexican people unless they're valeting your car or doling out canapes. My bad." He bowed his head in sarcastic apology, then looked around the room. "Ooo, speaking of which..."

He snapped his fingers and pointed to the trays of snack food and stack of pizza boxes through the hallway in the dining room, then casually waltzed over to them.

The guy who was throwing the party—a boring, fairly nice guy named Spencer who I used to be a lot closer to—followed after him. The circle of people around me turned back toward each other and resumed their conversations, silently deciding to ignore all unexpected intrusions on their routine.

I was bored with them, so I got up and went to watch Spencer trying to throw Gabriel out.

"C'mon man," Spencer said, aiming for reason. "I don't wanna have to kick you out."

"And I appreciate that, thanks buddy."

Gabriel patted Spencer on the back and went back to stacking pizza on a paper plate balanced over the expensive whiskey glass he'd just swiped.

"I'm asking you to please leave," Spencer said sternly. Gabriel frowned at him.

"Oh, I'm wounded!" he whined. Then his expression turned back to casual indifference. "But don't worry, I'll head out as soon as I redistribute your wealth a little bit. You won't even notice."

He winked and smiled.

Another boy, a wrestler who'd been hanging out in the kitchen leaning against the sink, said, "Get the fuck out, buddy. It's us against you."

"Oh shit, sorry, bro!" Gabriel said, not deigning to even look at him. "I didn't mean to interrupt your Aryan race workshop."

The wrestler approached Gabriel, tried to intimidate him by encroaching on his personal space. Gabriel was totally unfazed.

"Yes, you're large. Your point?"

The wrestler flipped Gabriel's paper plate over. Four slices of olive and mushroom fell face down on the floor.

Gabriel isn't the strongest or most agile person in the world. He's tall, but not especially tall. He doesn't play any sports, at least not officially. But the advantages he has always had are his element of surprise, people consistently underestimating him, and his willingness to fight dirty.

Gabriel looked down at the pizza, looked at the wrestler, then went to smash his whiskey glass against the wrestler's head. The wrestle avoided this, ducking his head just in time. The glass left Gabriel's hand and flew across the room, shattering against the wall. Apparently, Gabriel had anticipated him missing, as in the next heartbeat, he slammed his foot into the wrestler's right leg, leaving him crumbled on the floor.

"What the FUCK, bro!" Spencer yelled, holding

onto the wrestler as he fell back. Gabriel took another slice of pizza from the box and took a bite casually while walking away.

"Oops!" He threw open the sliding back door and ran off.

"I'll go after him," I said calmly, more interested than offended.

"Teach that fuckin' kid a lesson!" the wrestler said. "Ah! Jesus, my leg." He pulled up his pant leg to look at the damage, crying that it felt like it was broken. Later, I would find out he only got a bad bruise.

I found Gabriel under a streetlight a couple blocks away, looking at the signs, a half-eaten slice still in his hand.

"Hey, Gabe," I said. He looked at me, nodded, and continued to eat his pizza. He never had the immediate disdain for me he had for other kids in my social circles, and proved this when he let me walk up to him.

"Sup?" he said, after swallowing a bite.

"Want to go somewhere?" I asked.

"With you?"

"Yeah, why not?"

He shrugged. "You're not really my type, is all."

"I didn't mean it like that," I said. "It's just, you didn't get to finish your drink back there."

"Hah! Good point."

"I've got the keys to Hyde's Place," I said. "We could hang out on the roof over there."

"What about your friends back there?"

I shrugged. "What friends?"

The rest, I guess, is history.

Jules and Gabriel. Maybe the only two people outside my family who mattered in my whole life, and they weren't even reliable friends. Maybe they were so distinct exactly because I only ever got to know them in glimpses. Find out too much about a person and you lose interest, right? Exotic outskirts stay more appealing than the bustling interior.

They were the only people in my life to speak honestly, to pour their hearts out and frankly reveal that they were trying, struggling, working out their own sets of problems, proving that people can be thoughtful and that life doesn't have to be full of forgettable conversations.

Far from perfect, delusional and selfish and crazy in their own ways.

But they were trying.

I put the absinthe on my desk, stuck the note in a shoe box that carries all the sentimental things I didn't have the heart to throw out: Childhood photos, a bracelet that once belonged to my mother, birthday cards from friends I'd lost touch with, postcards from Gordon on the European backpacking trips he used to go on every summer, a post-it note that Jules had doodled Buffy Summers on and slapped onto my back between classes one day, Gabriel's letter…

High school was almost over, I realized.

These dear, precious influences on my life, too abstract to call friends, would be leaving soon anyway.

I didn't have a thing to do.

No obligations, no promises, no ties really.

After graduation, I would work, keep myself occupied with a humble, hectic little job, and figure out what the hell else I was supposed to do with myself.

I saved the absinthe but found another drink for myself elsewhere.

8 – The undrunk glass of absinthe

Through the grapevine of high school gossip, I found out that Jules' little brother had gotten suspended for fighting. The story was that Joshua had taken a swing at another kid in the cafeteria during lunch, and the other kid had shoved Joshua to the ground. After the ensuing administrative intervention, Joshua was sentenced to three days' suspension, while the other kid served two hours of detention for fighting back.

Joshua.

I'd completely neglected him once he had told me about what had happened with Jules. It should have been so obvious to reach out to him. Who else could I talk to about her? Joshua must miss Jules in a way I could not even imagine. I hated myself for only now realizing that.

In thinking about her, in wanting her, I'd dehumanized Jules, forgot her earthly ties, forgot that people other than me were connected to her. She became a concept in my head. She told me so many times how much Joshua meant to her, how she felt like he was the only person she could ever trust completely, and I never considered taking that into account. I should have talked to him months ago, should have checked up at least. We didn't know each other too well, only talked a few times, but we both felt a certain way about her being gone, right? Who better to lean on, to confide in about how much I could not help but miss this girl?

I had his number, but had some trouble figuring out how to go about texting him. I elected to go with my old strategy of getting slightly drunk, spending way too much time typing up an awkward message and pressing SEND before I had any time to think about it.

[We should talk sometime. Doesn't have to be about the suspension, that's whatever. About Jules. We should have talked months ago.]

He responded in about an hour:

[ok, we can talk]

It was difficult, judging by these words, to figure out how he felt. It could have been apprehension or enthusiasm or begrudging agreement. We would meet at least. We planned to meet outside his house in about an hour.

I pulled up to the curb and saw Joshua sitting on his doorstep, one arm propped on his leg, fist squeezed into his cheek, the other hand holding a phone, thumb absentmindedly twiddling. He wore a black hoodie and cargo shorts. He waited for me to get out of the car and I waited for him to approach it. A few moments passed, unsure if we were walking or driving. The two of us separately realized this and left our respective perches, meeting in the middle of the yard.

Joshua looked no more disgruntled than I expected any teenage boy in his situation to look.

"Do you want to go somewhere?" I asked.

He shrugged.

The onset of summer brought a heavy warmth to the roof of Hyde's Place. That midwestern humidity that never fully leaves in the summer, not even in the dead of night.

Below us inside the bar, middle-aged men and

117

women—tired and calm and merry, smiling and conversing—listened to live country music, a local duo of salt-and-pepper-haired old men who loved to play and played for cheap. The music rose, murmurs seeping through the ceiling.

I prepared Gabriel's absinthe—placed a sugar cube on a slotted spoon over both glasses, poured water over them, and watched the green liquid bloom into yellow.

"Do you usually drink?" I asked, setting the spoons aside and handing him a glass.

"Not anymore," he said, as if he were in recovery. Then I remembered.

"Jules told me, actually, that you and her used to drink a lot," I said.

"Yeah." Then, as if the levees broke, he opened up to me. "Some stuff happened when we were in middle school that was kinda hard to communicate about," he explained, "and there was this person she got it from… It helped us talk, I think. I only ever drank with her though. We haven't for a long time."

"Yeah, she also cryptically alluded to something happening to you two."

He didn't take the bait, but deflected.

"So why do you drink so much?"

"Okay, is my reputation really that bad?"

"Kind of." Joshua shrugged. "You used to be a hot topic around school. But nobody really talks about you anymore. Kinda dropped off the face of the earth."

"Hm," I said, thinking about how to take that. "Well, drinking is a family thing. I grew up with a lot of heavy drinkers. I like the taste. But also, in terms of being social, I guess I do it for the same reason you and Jules drank. It's really difficult to talk to people. Like, to really honestly talk to them about what they want to talk about, what's really on their mind. It's sort of a shortcut."

"Eh, I've heard that argument," Joshua said, leaning his head to one side. "I think that's just the fear of connecting with people openly."

"But what about you and Jules?" I countered.

"Are you really advocating for preteens to get drunk to help talk through their trauma?"

"I, uh, I didn't think of it like that."

"Just because it happened to work out okay for us doesn't mean it's supposed to," Joshua explained. "We got lucky, is all. But seriously, if you're not afraid of connecting with another person, it shouldn't be that hard to just... talk."

"If you're a stronger person than me, probably."

"Jules doesn't like to drink," he said, shifting the conversation. "She told me she saves it for special conversations, when she wants to say something, but doesn't trust herself to say it under, y'know, more normal circumstances."

Facts aligned in my head. Jules had drunk with me that night in the fall. Right here, right on this roof. And if Jules only drank when she wanted to say something important, to unabashedly connect with another human being... I looked back on that night. Had she said what she had wanted to say? Had we connected? Or had she lost interest? Or had it been Dennis, his intrusion on our one-on-one, who prevented her from doing so?

Joshua and I talked, bonded maybe. I told him about my family's little empire, all the bars and restaurants, the culinary enthusiasm, the alcohol connoisseurs. He told me about himself, how he'd been dealing with Jules being gone.

"It's not bad," he said. "It's just... I've been repressing my feelings a little. But she needs to do what she needs to do."

We talked about old sci-fi movies. He gave a good lecture on what *Silent Running* had to say about environmental conservation, and we discussed whether it'd be good or bad to live in the world of *Logan's Run*. He made some pointed remarks about how much he disliked Heinlein and Asimov.

He didn't have Jules' extroversion, I noticed. Conversations flowed disjointedly with him. Topics hit brick walls faster than I expected them to. Answers came without further elaboration. It wasn't bad, it just took some extra effort on my part to pick up the slack. Joshua didn't have his sister's gift for making people feel welcome and happy. He spoke in critiques, and often spoke like he was figuring the topic out for himself, not explaining it to someone else.

I noticed some similarities, though. He had her sense of humor, very deadpan and sarcastic. And though he wasn't warm and open like her, I could still feel his appreciation for my company. Something about the way he talked and looked at me.

My glass was almost gone.

His remained almost entirely full.

He drank out of politeness, in little sips.

Absinthe isn't exactly a usual flavor, so I could hardly hold it against him.

"Okay," I said, "I have to know. Why did you punch that guy?"

He sighed in that way only misunderstood teenagers can sigh.

"Well," he said, "it's stupid but... well you know most of what happened, right?"

"You socked a dude in the cafeteria."

"Yeah, sure. That's about the size of it. He said some things and... I don't know. He wasn't being any meaner than usual. Guys like him are often picking on me, whatever. I don't get angry. It doesn't build up like it does with other people. But I've been really anxious lately. Or angry with myself or something. Or like, I'm tired of being me. So basically, I just did something un-me-like."

"Because of Jules being gone?"

"Part of it. I miss her and all. But it's more... it's more what happened in the fall. With Dennis. Why she left, not that she's gone. Although that didn't help."

"Mind explaining more?"

He sighed again.

"A boy I knew killed himself. He made the conscious decision to end his life. Doesn't that bother you?"

I nodded.

"Of course."

"Of course. But how often do you think about it? Talk about it? Nobody talks about it. Everyone just assumes that life is worth living no matter what, and that what he did was the objectively wrong thing to do. A terrible tragedy, sure, but still wrong. They say stuff like 'a permanent solution to a temporary problem.' But it's not that simple. They don't get it."

"People are sensitive about that stuff."

"Whatever. When someone dies, all everybody else can do is reaffirm life for themselves. They don't understand that it's not about them. A boy killed himself. Someone with food and water and shelter, who lives in a more or less peaceful community, can still kill himself. That should haunt them. But instead, Dennis just caused a little stir for a few weeks and then they moved on. Nobody thinks about him. Not really, anyway. They're going to remember him when it's his birthday; they'll post things on Instagram about missing him. And then go on with their lives a minute later."

"What do you suggest then?"

"Nothing, nothing… Except, like, stuff like this should force us to try harder, be better. Like, neither of us are currently killing ourselves. We should be asking why. But you bring up the question, and all it does is shock and scare and upset people."

"So you've been obsessing over death ever since."

"Yes."

"Thoughts so far? Why haven't you decided life isn't worth living?"

He shrugged again.

"I guess I haven't experienced enough to judge. Like, right now, personally… there are things I like. I like cooking with my sister, reading books… I wanna help the environment. Stuff like that. There are things I want to know more about, things I want to do. Maybe something will happen to me that'll make finding things out and doing things with them irrelevant, but for the time being, my experiences tell me to keep going."

I tried to pick apart his words in my head. I didn't know where to begin.

"And you," Joshua continued. "What takes suicide off the bill for you?"

"Oh, well." My answer was ready-made. "Because I have it too good. I don't have problems. With the position I'm in, it's my obligation to observe and appreciate others, and help in whatever way I can if necessary."

"Isn't there something messed up about living solely for the sake of other people? I hate that argument, how you're not supposed to kill yourself just because other people will be sad."

"Yeah. It's not the same though. I have the means and the willingness to accomplish something. I don't know what, is all."

"That's something."

"Yeah. It's something."

"I guess Dennis didn't have that."

"He wanted to be anywhere but here and took an exit."

Joshua sat quietly awhile. He drew up his legs, hugged his knees. I saw the resemblance to Jules there somewhere. His glass was still half-full. It didn't look like he'd be having any more.

"Have you heard from her since she left?" I asked.

"No," he said. "You?"

"No," I said. "I miss her."

"I bet she'd miss you too if she gave herself any amount of time to think about it."

I smiled, raised my glass to him in approval. Then we sat in companionable silence for a while.

"It's nice up here," he commented.

"Nicest place in the world," I said.

"There's one more thing," Joshua added some time later, as if deciding it was time, "that I haven't told anyone but Jules."

"Oh?"

"About… about Dennis."

His voice got shaky, nervous. He was about to say something big. It was the labor of digging out a buried truth, of revealing it to someone who he did not absolutely trust with the information, unlike his sister.

I could have egged him on. Instead I let him finish on his own time.

"I'm pretty sure I'm the reason he did it."

9 - Joshua's letter, or apologies to the dead

(Truth telling is a funny thing. That one simple, declarative statement, admitting what he knew about Dennis to me, caused it all to come pouring out. All of a sudden, Joshua went from reserved to relying on me for help. He needed a way to collect and organize this information, to make sense of it. These past few months had left so many things swimming in his head. Jules could listen, but she couldn't help him. She had too much of her own baggage to deal with.

Joshua and I collaborated on the following. We spent every evening the next week together, cooking dinner then hanging out in my basement, talking in rounds, taking breaks in between by watching old episodes of Star Trek.

He spoke at length. I asked questions for clarity, transcribed, and finally edited this.)

I was the great love of Dennis's life. That's the big secret. Maybe people know at this point. Maybe someone has gone through his diaries, checked his messages. But nobody else knows the way that I know. Nobody was the subject of his feelings the way that I was.

There are so many stories about wanting to be with someone. Stories about a faraway object of desire, some more perfect-than-life person eternally out of the protagonist's reach. There is not a lot about being the one who's wanted. And like, it makes sense. The feeling of pure, desperate yearning is much juicier to read about than the complicated, unsympathetic perspective of the beloved who does not and will not and cannot love the same way back.

That's me. That's my role in this story.

Being the object of desire always seems to be construed as a kind of power in stories. We tend to root for people who don't have all the power, who work against the odds to achieve their goals. But the interplay of loving and being loved isn't power. It's more complicated. I didn't hold anything over Dennis, didn't manipulate him. I cared about him. But he put me into a position where I had no course of action to take except to hurt him.

Dennis was my friend. I loved him as a friend. I told him as much multiple times, even though I didn't want to explicitly say it. I knew it would send him even further down the path of wanting me in a way I couldn't return. But too many times, getting heartbroken texts and calls from him, hearing about how sad and lonely he was, telling him I loved him was all I could do to cheer him up.

We met in middle school, became friends the way kids in middle school become friends. It just happened. We had sleepovers, played videogames, went to movies. We rarely had heart-to-hearts, barely talked that deeply about anything. Honestly, I'm not even sure now how much we had in common. We were companions. I didn't, I don't, have many friends, and neither did he. Sometimes people bond over shared loneliness.

I'm not sure when it began, but at some point his feelings for me shifted.

When I couldn't hang out for whatever reason, he

Bryan Cebulski

started to say things like… like check out this text for
example:

[thats ok, just wanted to see you is all :)]

Like not wrong, exactly. Just not a normal thing
to say to your friend. Like, of course you feel the impulse to see your friend on occasion. They wouldn't be
your friend otherwise. But you don't just say it, not so
directly. Not with the subtextually rich smiley face. Not
when you're a thirteen-year-old boy, that golden age
when we're being taught by boy scout leaders and soccer
coaches to relentlessly suppress our feelings and treat everything like it's survival of the fittest. That vulnerability
and sincerity are weaknesses.

I point that one text out in particular because I
found it weird at the time and took a screenshot. I'm
glad I did. Now I keep it as a reminder.

The funny, infuriating thing is, I don't know what
kind of friends we would be to each other now. I don't
know what kind of friends we would have been to each
other then either, if he hadn't felt the way he did about
me. He had the potential to always be my best friend,
someone who I clicked with more and more as we aged.
He also had the potential to be someone who slowly re-
ceded from my life for no other reason than it happened
to be that way.

It felt like I barely even knew him when it comes
down to it. I knew facts about him. Family, hobbies,
dreams. I knew the experiences we shared. I knew the
sound of his voice, the shape of his face.

But did I really know him? And if I had, would that
have made a difference? Is it exactly because I was unable to really get to know him that I couldn't feel the

127

same way back? That I felt no desire to feel that way?

Fuck, man.

Dennis liked sci-fi too. It's the main way we bonded. Although I could tell he never liked it in the same way. He didn't like it for the visions of a better future, of dreaming about new worlds, of becoming better than humanity in its current form. I know he really liked astronomy, but it was always a sort of admiration of beauty thing for him. Like, he loved looking at the stars, loved how patterns looked in the sky. He didn't especially care about astrophysics. He appreciated the aesthetics more than anything, the neon art direction, that fusion of style and tech. Which, like, obviously I appreciate that too, but... now I wonder sometimes if he even liked that stuff that much, or if watching sci-fi TV shows and movies was merely a means of getting close to me and he found whatever he could to enjoy about them to accomplish that.

That's what I mean, did I know him? I'm doubting everything. Did I only know the person he was trying to be, the one he was desperately hoping I would like?

I'm certain of a few things. Like how he wanted to be more fashion conscious, but was too afraid to try more aggressively. I only think of this because he always used to comment on the clothes people were wearing in the movies we watched, before anything else.

He would also say things like "Oh, I would love to be able to pull something like that off." And I'd ask why not try and he'd get shy and go "It probably wouldn't look good on me."

So it was always this mix of plain clothes and slightly better than normal grooming, like cleaning under his nails and combing his hair with more purpose than just raking through it with your fingernails.

Anyway. I'd prefer to just wallow in abstractions without actually addressing what I came here to talk about, but fine. I'll move on to what happened.

The first time I knew for sure was one night during a sleepover at his place, in the basement. I was asleep on the couch, or at least he thought I was asleep. I'm pretty sure he was awake the whole night. I could tell something was up, so I pretended to sleep and kept a watch on him, my eyes nearly closed. He paced in front of me as if trying to prep himself to say something to me.

He shook me awake at one point. I pretended it didn't work.

Then, later, I felt him looming over me. Not in a threatening way. At least, I didn't get that feeling. Not to excuse him, I mean it's creepy on paper, creepy to an extent to me too, I guess. But he didn't have a threatening aura, or whatever. I could just tell that he only wanted to be close to me and that this was the only time he could think of doing it without thinking I noticed.

In the morning, I acted like nothing had happened. So did he.

It wasn't until about a week later when I decided to actually confront him about it. Or, confront is too strong a word. I'm not an especially confrontational person. More like, open up the discussion.

It was almost the same scene, late at night in his basement.

In theory, I thought of saying something along the lines of, "I'm not a fucking idiot, Dennis, what's going on?" In execution, it came out more like "Uh... Dennis,

I, um, I just wanted to ask… it's just that you seem to, I don't know how to say it, and like don't be offended… I mean you're my friend, like, I mean… please don't be mad but it seems like you… maybe like me more than that?"

At first, he denied it, pretended to be offended, stormed off, and I ended up going home early that night. He didn't speak to me for a couple days. Then he wrote me a letter and stuck it into my backpack when I wasn't looking at school one day.

It wasn't much of a surprise. Like I've mentioned, it was pretty obvious. Only I wasn't sure what to do. I asked Jules about it and we spent the night going over the options. Ignoring was out of the question. Curt but polite text message, Jules' preferred option, wasn't really in my wheelhouse.

Actually, the night shifted from my course of action to Jules asking me how I could take this all in so casually. And that's when we started to have a different conversation.

Here's the thing about me that I've come to terms with since this whole thing started: I do not feel attraction to anyone. Not romantic, not anything. Accepting it was a long time in the making. Like obviously, I have types of people I prefer to hang out with, but I've never had any motivation for dating or sex or anything. None. I guess I like the idea of cuddling a little bit, but otherwise I'm not even curious. Maybe it'll be different with the right person, but right now, it's just genuinely outside my interests.

So it didn't freak me out, Dennis admitting his feelings for me. Because my not being able to understand how someone could have those feelings in the first place felt as weird and socially unacceptable to me as having them for another guy.

We made plans to talk at my house with Jules in the next room on standby, just in case, well, I'm not sure in case of what. In case I needed emotional support I guess. I didn't question the arrangement at the time.

So we sat in the living room and talked—without drinking, if you can believe it. Fucking shocking, I know. Scandalous, really.

I said what you would expect me to say. That I was flattered, but didn't feel the same way about him. Not into guys that way, or anyone for that matter. But I'm there for you as a friend if you need me.

It seemed like Dennis took this all well at the time. He cried and he thanked me for being direct and honest. I waited for him to finish crying, and we ended up playing videogames all night.

And then I... I mean, it's not like I actively tried to stop being his friend. But I started to become more and more convinced that he wasn't really friends with me because we had anything in common. And even that wasn't like I was completely wrong. It's impossible to know how much for real, but at the time, it became clearer and clearer to me that we only hung out because he liked me. In hindsight, maybe I was a little freaked out, over-exaggerating the extent to which he hung out with me purely out of affectionate aims.

But also in my defense, we never talk about how much of a betrayal it can feel like when your friend admits they like you. It throws your whole relationship into a different context. There's this fridge horror effect, where you realize the things you thought were just awkward had deeper implications. And I don't blame him for that. He clearly didn't have enough support somewhere else in his life. It just fucking sucks that he had to dump all his issues on me, build me up as this person who could complete him in some way. Because I sure as hell couldn't handle it. It was like a train headed into a brick wall, the way he kept hoping that someday, I would understand and return his feelings.

Like, shockingly I had my own things to deal with? I was also thirteen and wildly confused about myself. I mean, I'm fifteen now and still confused. I had my birthday by myself in December, by the way. Thanks, man. No, I mean, it's fine. I'm fine. I don't know why I mentioned that.

The fact is, when you realize you only have one friend and that this friend isn't really your friend in the same way back; that in fact, they have this weird expectation of you that you can never fulfill for them… that can mess you up! Like, really badly!

So like I said, I started slowly distancing myself from him. Gradually stopped being able to hang out. Can't make it to a sleepover this weekend, yeah darn, sorry. No that movie sounds good, but I don't think I can make it to the theater after school tomorrow, maybe another time. And when he asked me if I was ignoring him, I denied it flatly. Don't be so paranoid, man. Really, Dennis, I'm sorry but I've been busy. Busy with, uh, stuff. Lots of stuff. Just piles of it. Heaps. Buried in stuff. No, no nothing you could help me with. But thanks, yeah no, really thank you. Maybe next week. Or the week after. Or the week after that. Eventually for sure. Promise!

Maybe you're asking yourself, how could you claim to care about your friend and treat them like that? Oh, you're not thinking that? Well the thought definitely crossed your mind at least. It crossed mine. And all I have to say to that is that it is very difficult to always enjoy the people you love. The idea is pretty solidly established for families, but it doesn't seem to carry over to friendships the same way. Like, my mom loves Jules and me, but she doesn't really like us. She's not interested in us as people, not interested in being active in our lives. But she provides for us, and somehow that's acceptable. Or at least, more understandable to society.

Okay, that's kind of different from what I'm trying to explain, but I guess there that is. Now you know a hint more about our fucked up family situation.

What I'm saying is, we've generally agreed that friendship, and especially friendship between guys, is this transient concept that no one necessarily needs to show any kind of loyalty to or respect for. You can leave a friendship at any time, scot-free. You can be horrible to your friends and the expectation is to get over it because they're just your friends.

Maybe it's my own stuff, but I've just never thought that way. Not at least for good friends. Not that I've had many, but, like, it means something to me that Dennis and I helped keep each other from being friendless and I wanted to honor that. But I couldn't cope with him acting the way that he did toward me either. And so I was torn between caring for him deeply in one respect and not being able to stand being around him at all in another.

It's not like we fought. It was just quiet cruelty.

Passive-aggression.

Acting like he was making things up when he started picking up on the fact that I was clearly actively ignoring him.

And then, eventually, we stopped hanging out altogether. This happened over the course of a few months. God, things move quickly. We texted on occasion, talked online, and Jules said he was doing the same with her, but that was about it for us. I didn't really follow up with him on how he felt about me. I hoped it would go away.

The other thing about this time is that I really gave a lot of thought to whether or not I could date Dennis. Like, I felt an urge to reciprocate. Like I was supposed to. To make him happy in that way, as some kind of reward for being my friend. The thought wasn't repulsive to me and I misconstrued that feeling as there being a chance. Like, his face was a face like any other. It was a nice face. I liked when he smiled. He had a good laugh. It was goofy, he could almost cluck with joy if you got him going enough. But then who doesn't like seeing your friends smile and laugh? And he wasn't that different from me physically. So it was like if I'm not disgusted looking at my body then why would I ever be disgusted with his?

I never told him, but I thought about him and me together. Really explored the idea. Way more than any straight boy would have, I can tell you that. And I guess the fact that I thought about it so much made me even more frustrated with him. Made me feel resentful that he'd knocked me into this quagmire and all of a sudden it was my responsibility to find a way out. Because at the end of the day, I couldn't make sense of the idea. Not for any reason I could follow logically. It just didn't feel right. Didn't work. That was all.

I didn't make new friends. That whole situation doesn't come easy to me. It's fine, again. No really, it is. Dennis meanwhile seemed to pick up these girls who liked him as an accessory. And who could blame him for accepting that role because really, those girls protected him. They slotted him into the social ecosystem in a way that other people could suddenly understand. Like, oh he's that one guy, you know, the one guy always surrounded by girls, but in a way that's nonthreatening to us heteros—is he... y'know? I mean maybe. No, let's be real, probably. But better to leave him alone even if he is, because if we beat the shit out of him, then word will get back to those girls and we want to fuck those girls, and if he tells them then they might not want to fuck us.

Maybe it's over judgmental or a weird, inconsistent possessiveness I had over him and our friendship. But he always seemed lonely still, even with all that attention. Even though he found a way to fit in.

There wasn't any big blowout fight leading to his death. At least, none I was a part of. No enormously consequential event.

What I do know is that he texted me that night.

[I love you and I miss you and I'm sorry] he said.

Which... honestly annoyed me more than anything at the time.

You have to understand, he texted me stuff like this fairly often. Every other weekend at least.

I'm pretty sure he started drinking a little bit, and I'm pretty sure whenever he did, I would get one of those texts. Texting that you love someone after a certain time of night on a weekend just kind of has an inherent drunk text energy to it, doesn't it?

The "I miss you" was unusual, though. He didn't really say that much. Typically he'd say "I love you" or "I really appreciate our friendship," even though if we ever got down to admitting it, very little of our friendship was left—but no "I miss you." Because that would indicate that we didn't hang out anymore. And we totally hung out—or, I mean, we *could* have hung out more. Things just kept coming up. Sorry, man! Really. I just keep putting it off, because I'm afraid of you, and I don't want someone who feels so strongly about me in my life, and it fucking sucks to feel like you owe someone something that you can't provide them.

Maybe we would have drifted even further apart and been like strangers to each other after a while. Maybe he would have gotten over his crush on me and found some other boy, and they could get together and we would all be friends, and we'd laugh about the way he used to feel about me. Who's to say?

I didn't go to the funeral. His parents actually called me and said I was welcome to if I wanted. Nobody would have really known me there, though. It freaked me out, the idea of being surrounded by his family; none of them understanding who I was or what my role had been. No. I haven't been to the grave yet either. I probably should. I haven't really had a way to get there without a car though.

I did go to that bullshit memorial service though. Stayed the whole time, quietly fuming by myself in the back corner. You left early, huh? Yeah, that was probably a good call. It didn't do anything. Didn't offer any kind of catharsis. Just made me angry. And I've been sitting with this anger ever since, completely unsure of what to do with it. I'll let you know when I figure it out.

Dennis was my friend and I loved him and now he's dead.

That's it. Yeah, that's all. I don't know what else to say. Except that I miss him too.

(I don't know what to do with this document. The only copy we printed is sitting somewhere in a drawer in Joshua's desk. Printed double-sided. Held together with a paper clip. I used Bookman Old Style font and one inch margins. I double spaced the lines.

For what it's worth, reading it seemed to help Joshua. To put everything into perspective.

We visited Dennis' grave as a sort of ritual punctuation to the whole project. Joshua kneeled in front of the stone marker embedded into the ground and cried.)

10 – Humble inadequacy

Even now, having written all this, it's hard to say when I went from troubled, but more or less stable to near-irreparably... What's the word? Out-of-control? Empty? Disconsolate? Numb? I don't know. But after those nights talking everything over with Joshua and writing out his story, I felt like I'd fallen off my tenuous balance over the abyss. The drinking got heavier, the loneliness more intense, the all-consuming existential woe ever more oppressive, until one night, I got more deeply drunk and lost than I had ever been before.

I leaned against a brick wall in an alleyway, tried not to dry heave. Held my phone to my ear and waited until I heard the beep.

"Hey dad," I said, trying to sound sober. Failing. "I'm... I'm not okay right now. Can you pick me up? I'm..."

I looked around and realized I didn't know where I was exactly. Could have sworn I was just at Hyde's Place. How could I not know where I was in a town with only a couple main streets? But everything blurred for me then. Lines of bars, cafes and pizza places, closed Christian bookstores and gas stations. The streets swerved and merged, identical strips of buildings transitioning into identical neighborhoods. Houses with lights on in the windows, looking eerie and haunted; disembodied eyes never helping, only judging, merely watching for disorder, calling in disruption. Then even this creepy in-human entity known as suburbia eventually petering out into cornfields and nothingness.

"You know what," I said, "never mind. I'll be home soon. I'll make my own way back."

I hung up.

My little hamlet loosely neighbored a small city with a university campus, about a twenty minutes' drive away. On the weekends, students poured into our bars and restaurants, ran rampant on the streets. Their faces merged with those of the kids I knew from school with fake IDs, soon to graduate and join their college student ranks for real.

I joined them, a stringer-on. Someone who would never move forward. There was nothing else for me to do. I hobbled from streetlight to streetlight, dizzy and tired and gross. A couple guys who looked like they were born by congealing in a puddle behind J. Crew went up to me, grabbed me by the arm and made me dance around with them, arms threaded together, swinging, until finally pushing me off, laughing and going back to their own conversation.

After I'd passed them by about a block, I pulled my phone out again and scrolled through my contacts.

He didn't pick up when I called. I waited for the beep.

"Hey Gabe," I said. "I'm, uh, I'm not doing great. But more I wanted to call to say..." Here I tried not to hiccup, failed. "Well, let me start by saying I've been through a lot more than I've ever been through before lately. And it just makes me realize that I miss you, and you're my friend, and I really wish we could get through the bull-shit and admit that to each other."

I grabbed a streetlight and swung around it, turned the corner into the unknown.

"Like, why are you such an asshole to me?" I asked.
"Obviously there's something about me you enjoy for us
to hang out as often as we used to. Like, is there something you don't want to admit to yourself about us? You
know what I mean. Is it because I'm not some fucking
freshman twink you can creep on? Sorry. I mean, I'm not
sorry. Call me if you want. Or keep being a shitty friend.
Whatever. Bye."

The neighborhood looked like the one where Jules
lived. But then so many of these neighborhoods did.
The nicer, quainter sections closer to downtown; the
older ranch-style homes built with character and spirit
well before McMansions like mine popped up in rings
around them.

It almost felt like home. A home. One I didn't have
but that I wanted.

I looked through my contacts, considered anyone
else I could bother. Estelle? Hell no. Jules? Hah. She'd
deleted all her social media and it was unlikely she regu-
larly checked her phone abroad. Joshua? I was there for
him lately, now he could be there for me. I felt tempted,
but the thought brought a pitiful lump to my throat. A
deep disappointment in myself settled in my stomach.
How, out of everyone, did I now find the little brother of
my crush, who I barely knew and who didn't need any
extra drama in his life, the only person in the world I
could trust to call?

Especially when his story was what had driven me
into feeling this incontrovertibly miserable in the first
place. No, his was only the last in a long line of experiences pushing me down into the gutter.

I liked Joshua. He was extremely smart and independent for his age. I did what I could to let him know that what had happened with Dennis wasn't his fault, as much as he seemed to blame himself for it. It was tough, because he didn't blame himself directly. It was more like a spiritual blame, something indescribably more tangible than the physical.

I don't know why I decided to get blindingly drunk and wander the streets past midnight. Does anyone? It's the thing you do when you're out of other options; when you feel so irrelevant to the universe, you do something extravagantly foolish just to feel something.

Or, no. Feeling nothing isn't accurate. It's what's expected of me, where the narrative always wants to drive the protagonist. Get them to the point where they're so jaded they can't feel anything anymore, too hardened and hollow. No, that isn't and wasn't me. To the contrary, I was too full of feeling. Too full of the experiences of everyone around me. Running the gamut of emotional outbursts. Flailing, trying to make sense of myself in the madness.

I called Gabriel again.

"You kept talking about *The Myth of Sisyphus*," I said after the beep. "Well, my obsessive text of choice is *The Great Gatsby*. Fuck off, I can absolutely hear you talking shit in my head right now. Just because it's an AP English cornerstone doesn't mean it's not good.

"Thing is, I keep thinking of myself as Nick. The passive narrator, the fly on the wall observing the lives of people more interesting than him. Only, Nick goes through so much in that goddamn book. Falls in love with some hot, rich asshole, only to find him dead in the pool. Murdered, thanks to the indifferent cruelty

141

of a friend, who the rich guy he was in love with, was obsessed with, and fucking the whole time. Because straight people cheating on each other is more important, more existentially rich with meaning, than queer people pining for someone. No wonder Nick winds up in an institution. I think I might do the same thing."

If you can say only one thing for the teenagers in my hometown, it is that they are consistent. I wandered from sidewalks to backyards and knew I would inevitably wander into a house party spilling out into a backyard, with a case of shitty beer leaning against the shed, just out of sight, and people I vaguely knew circled around a fire on tattered lawn chairs.

They nodded to me, either not noticing how completely fucked up I looked or politely ignoring it, with a round of "Sup man!"s and "Yo"s from guys who wore backward baseball caps. I stumbled into a lawn chair, letting smoke billow into my face. Someone tossed a can of beer into my lap. I popped the tab and drank.

"You ever gotten laid, dude?" one guy in a torn-up sleeveless shirt asked me seemingly out of nowhere. Though bragging about sex was a continuous conversation between these types of guys.

I nodded.

"A girl, right?" another asked, launching the group into laughter.

I shook my head.

"Oh. Dude then?" the second one followed-up. "That's cool, bro. My uncle's gay. That's chill."

I shook my head again. "Not that either."

They got confused. One of the less tactful bros suggested I'd probably fucked a dog, then another one pointed out dogs have gender too, then they started accusing each other of being dog fuckers, until eventually, they got bored of the game and moved on to another subject.

"Yo, pass me the human," sleeveless shirt asked another of his cohorts. This seemed an odd sentence. Someone tossed him a water bottle. I remembered then, a burgeoning slang developing among the athletic-leaning population at school that made very little sense: They used "human" for food, water, clothing, necessities like that, and "non" for unessential items. Splitting everything in existence into only two categories was a bold move, but they seemed to figure it out through context clues. In PE, for example, if you were shooting hoops and you heard someone say "Pass me the non," inevitably someone else would toss them a basketball. Then, later after the game, they'd say "Give me some human," and they'd get water or a protein bar. It was stupid enough to be slightly brilliant.

The others around the fire continued to say things to me and I said things back. I don't remember what they were. At one point, I asked for some "human," just to try it out, and found a water bottle dropped into my lap a second later.

Then I asked for a "non" to see what they'd think of first. Someone passed me a blanket. I draped it over my lap.

I leaned my head back, looked at the night sky through smoky air and passed out.

When I woke, some hours later, the party had collected itself back into the house. I was shivering. The blanket was gone. The fire smoldered, embers the color of honey.

I stretched my feet, felt my toes dig into grass. I looked down and saw that my shoes were missing. I checked my back pocket. So was my wallet. I checked a front pocket. And my phone.

I froze in place, conscious, but unable to motivate myself to get up. Like my body instinctively resisted admitting that I was a flesh and blood human inhabiting reality, that had to participate in this mortal existence.

"You okay?" I heard someone say.

Through bleary eyes, I saw Joshua walking toward me. He stood in front of me in the dark. Black hoodie, black beanie, as usual.

"Sup dude!" I said, laughing to myself. As if trying to play this off as casual.

He didn't say anything.

"Why're you here?" I asked, far more sober after waking. "Doesn't seem like your crowd."

"You texted me," he said.

"Oh." I stretched to make sense of my limbs. "I don't remember."

"No shit." He sighed. "Are you okay?"

"Not really," I said. A weight dropped in me. What a fucked up thing to do, bringing him into whatever bullshit I was going through here. "Sorry, I don't know why I messaged you. You can go if you'd rather."

"I'm not about to leave you like this," he said. Then he noticed. "What happened to your shoes?"

I shrugged.

"Fuck," he said. "Get up, man. I'm taking you home."

I shook my head.

"I don't want to go home right now."

He sighed again, more aggravated this time.

"Well, you're not staying here. Get up, you can crash in my basement."

"I should find my phone and wallet."

"You lost those too?" He looked exasperated with me already. He turned on the flashlight on his phone and started scanning the grass.

"Yeah. At least, I woke up without them."

He stopped searching and turned off his flashlight.

"Okay, that's different," he said. "That's called being robbed. It's much harder to find things that have been robbed from you."

"Makes sense," I said with a hiccup.

"I'm going to ask again: Can you get up?"

I tried my legs out. They worked. Shaky and numb, but they worked.

I followed him out through the alley between houses and back onto the street.

"Where's your car?" I asked, looking around.

"You remember I'm fifteen, right?"

Right. Being reminded of his age, that someone three years younger than me had his shit way more together than I did; that I was leaning on him for support at the moment, made me feel even worse.

"Sorry," I said.

"My house is only a few blocks away," he told me. "If you weren't so fucked up, you might've remembered that. Be extremely quiet when we get there, okay? My mom is asleep."

"Thanks, Joshua," I said.

"Don't mention it," he said. "Like, really don't."

We waded between streetlights, single family homes with all the insides dark, motion detector lights on their front porches blinking as we passed. No one else was out. Cars passed very rarely.

"How did you find me, anyway?" I asked.

"You said, and I quote loosely, that you were in the backyard at some bullshit party in some bullshit neighborhood and you fucking hated everyone there. And then for some reason, you pointed out that it's the only two-story home on McPherson Street and it's painted a, and I quote directly, 'godawful stupid washed out cream yellow.' "

"Oh," I said. "I mean, that yellow part is true. But thanks for tracking me down."

"Please stop thanking me. I'm mad at you."

"Okay. Sorry."

We went around to the back of his house and opened the sliding door, then tiptoed down to the basement. The light was already on downstairs. He guided me the whole way to make sure I didn't stumble in the dark.

The basement was two large rooms and a tiny bathroom. The one room further back looked like it was used for storage, the water heater, washer and dryer, all those out of the way household items.

The other was carpeted and lined with an L-shaped couch, centering on an old TV with half a dozen video game consoles hooked up to it. The TV was on, paused on some anime.

"You can sleep here," he said, pointing to the longer half of the couch.

"What are you watching?" I asked.

"An old Gundam series I pirated," he answered.

"Can I watch too?"

"You should sleep, I think."

"I think I'll feel better if I just fall asleep with it on."

"Fine. I wanted to finish this episode anyway. Just give me a sec."

He ran upstairs and came back down some moments later with a big glass of water and a box of crackers.

"Alright, take these, eat, drink, don't be merry." He handed me the glass and the box. "My mom goes to work early tomorrow and she almost never comes downstairs, so you're better off just staying here till nine or so."

"Aye-aye, cap'n," I said.

Joshua took off his beanie and tossed it on his section of the couch.

"But before we call it good for the night, I'm going to say one last thing." He stood over me, a hand to his hip and another scratching the back of his head, as if fishing around for the words. "Get help, man. Seriously. You need it. I'm so grateful for you helping me work out what I went through, but like, come on. We've barely met and you're supposed to be an adult. I can't be the only person you can rely on like this. Please."

I nodded.

Nobody had really told me that so directly before.

"I will," I said, fighting back the lump in my throat by stuffing my mouth with a fistful of crackers.

"Good." He sat back down on the couch. "Do you

want some context for the show?"

"Yeah," I said. "Although I feel like any time I watched one of these, it doesn't matter, because it still didn't make sense."

"That's true for some of them, but not this one."

"Alright, what's it about?"

"A race of humans from the moon is trying to recolonize Earth, right?" Joshua started, enthusiasm all of a sudden reinvigorating him.

We ended up going through at least six episodes before I fell asleep. I could barely keep my eyes open enough to read the subtitles. The music was nice though, and the sound of foreign voices keeping my consciousness occupied, kept the thoughts from forming a tempest in my head.

In the morning, very late in the morning, if the analog clock on the wall was accurate, a fat, short-haired gray cat with a tiny head walked over my chest to my face and meowed at me. I assume to demand food. I pet her once or twice, then she hopped off of me, continually looking back to me from the base of the stairs.

I walked upstairs. The cat led me into the kitchen to her bowl, where she went back and forth between staring at me and the bowl, meowing pointedly on occasion. You could see the bottom of the bowl, but it still had a ring of food in it.

"Ignore her," I heard Joshua say.

He was sitting by himself at the table, watching something on his laptop while eating toast with a steaming mug of light-colored tea.

"I fed her at her normal breakfast time, but she always tries tricking people into thinking she hasn't ever been fed in her life."

I tried petting the cat one more time, but she hissed and ran away. Looking at Joshua, realizing the life I had interrupted last night, I was reminded that I should be feeling incredibly ashamed of myself. With the added clarity of sobriety, it felt so much more powerful than the night before.

My head had nails in it.

My stomach felt like it had been melted in acid.

"There's coffee in the pot on the counter," he said. "And you can use my phone to call someone to pick you up, if you need it." He slid a small smartphone with a cracked screen across the table to me.

As I grabbed a mug from the counter, I tried to remember my father's number.

After a couple of misfires, I managed to get a hold of him. He hadn't gotten my voicemail until this morning, and thankfully, had only spent a couple hours worrying. He sounded disappointed, but not angry. Almost, I was sad to find, only irritated that I'd interrupted his Sunday morning. I knew him well enough to know he didn't like being parental; took for granted my more or less typically low-key behavior. I gave him the address after Joshua reminded me what it was. He said he'd pick me up soon.

"My mom heard you snoring this morning," Joshua said.

"Oh, shit."

"It's okay. She just assumed that I snuck a boy in."

"That's... good, then?"

Joshua shrugged.

"Easier than trying to explain that the guy who's in love with my sister was dead drunk, and I was the only one without a social life enough to respond to his texts."

"Sorry." I couldn't think of anything else to say. "Did I... I said something about Jules, huh?"

"Seriously? No, she's just told me about it. And you're not that hard to read anyway, dude."

"Oh. Well, are you and your mom cool, then?"

"Yeah, she always suspected anyway."

"But it's not true."

"I mean, backpedaling from the assumption that I'm gay or straight is the same to me. So I'm about where I was to begin with."

I tried not to laugh at his blasé attitude; the deadpan delivery of his reasoning.

"You've got a good way of looking at things," I admitted.

I poured myself a coffee and sat across the table from Joshua. He turned his video back on, something that sounded like a nature documentary, and we sat awhile, him watching, me listening. I watched the steam rise from the coffee, tried to ward off the hollowed-out feeling of a hangover.

"Could I use your laptop for a second?" I finally asked.

Joshua nodded while chewing his toast, paused the video, turned his laptop around and pushed it toward me.

I went on Instagram, logged him out while noting his handle to follow later, and logged myself in.

"What're you doing?" he asked.

"Finding help," I said, typing Lana's name into the search bar. "Like you said to."

When I heard my dad pull up to the driveway, Joshua stood up with me and said goodbye at the door.

"You're going to be okay, right?" he asked.

I shrugged.

"I'll try."

He smiled and suddenly wrapped his arms around me. It surprised me. I automatically started to hug him back, but said without thinking,

"Where did this come from?"

"I don't know," he said, retreating from the contact. "Seemed like something you'd like."

"Well, thanks, I guess." I wasn't sure how to take that and changed gears. "Let me know how, uh, reverse coming out to your mom goes."

Joshua laughed at that.

"I'll be fine. Take care of yourself, okay?"

"Okay."

11 – Jules' letter, or everyone is leaving

(On the day his suspension ended, as I was about to head to the classroom where Lana discreetly held her unofficial after-school queer group, Joshua found me by my locker. He held an envelope and gave it to me. It was addressed to his house, but had my name on it. The envelope was stuffed with folded paper.

"I got one too," he said. "Guess she finally took the time to miss us."

"Thank you," was all I managed to mumble, still processing what I was now holding.

"Mine's bigger than yours, by the way," Joshua said.

He shyly smiled as he walked away.)

Okay. My first and most lasting feeling toward you is that while you're a fun person, sometimes a good person, often an interesting person... I never want to speak to you again.

It's not out of hate. It's just that you're part of one book and that book's over.

Or no, that's lame. Fuck. No metaphors.

Look, I've just got to move on from that damn town. My life there was over long before I realized it. I have to move on from every single bit of it, including you. As much as I've enjoyed our time together, I've especially got to move on from you.

It took a lot to take this step. The only reason I pulled it off was because I didn't ever stop to think. Just did it. I still feel like I'm in that rush, sometimes. I wrote a letter to my brother to let him know how I'm doing, apologize for leaving him like that. And in the process of all that rambling, I found myself slowing down. Catching up. Having to deal with all that shit I've been escaping from. Realizing that despite the fact that I've spent a lot of time trying to convince myself I'm not who I was back in that town, that there's still the inextricable link of time linking me to her. She is me and I am her, as much as I've been avoiding it.

I'm not ready to address who I am yet, so here's where I am: I'm in a seaside town in the south of France. The tourists are here at last. People seem to think it's a bad time to vacation during fall and winter, but the weather was pretty nice overall. Fair and cool, though rainy enough to show the change of seasons. But some days there was just pure beautiful sunshine.

I liked it right off the bat. Except I got homesick a lot. Not for home as a location, but for my brother, even my mom. For the comfort of being in a place you've been in, know the routines of, you know? But even that sickness wasn't so bad. It was a sort of sweet sadness. "Bittersweet" doesn't quite match. Or maybe the word has been used too much; read it in too much bad teen girl poetry. Maybe it would fit if I could remove it from all of its contexts and associations.

Words are like putty rolling along, huh? They absorb everything they come into contact with.

Fuck. So much for no metaphors.

Anyway, the French must have a similar word for it. "Tristesse" is a good one. Like "sad," but in black-and-white, drinking espresso with a cigarette hanging out of its mouth. They're all about wallowing in moody bullshit here, as long as it's captured on celluloid in a pretty way. Must be why I feel good here. Like I'm among my people. Making progress or something.

Over fall and winter I helped out on a small organic farm on the outskirts of town. Mostly in the greenhouses, helping with harvests. I didn't like that so much, because the food just went to super bougie restaurants or farmers markets with over-inflated prices. But after a few weeks of that, since I was such a slow, shitty worker, they started to pass me around town to help elderly residents with their gardens. That was better. I liked seeing their homes and feeling that neighborly feeling despite the fact that we could barely understand one another. But even that was still too much hard work for me. I like what I'm doing now the best.

The tourists love their gelato. That's my job now. They decided I was too good as a public-facing person to waste behind the scenes. Jules, resident gelato cart girl.

It's actually unironically great.

They've got a good community here, like nothing I've seen anywhere else. Can you imagine, walking from your home, going to a cafe, getting a cup of coffee and drinking it on a deck overlooking a rocky beach and the bluest water you've ever seen? I don't think this place is typical, even for France, actually. I like it a lot. I'm not getting the full "French experience" maybe, but it's something different and new. It's what I wanted, something different.

Anyway, gelato. Creamier than ice cream. Less air pockets. That's basically what I say when tourists ask me what the difference is. I know it's not French! It's Italian!

I don't know what to tell you. These gelato carts just appear out of thin air in tourist spots. No one knows where they come from. Question it and you are carried off into the darkness, never to be seen again.

Tourists don't seem to care about the whole cultural disconnect thing though. It's mainly an English-speaking or English-as-second-language crowd anyway, which makes things easier for me. It's a good gig. Repetitive, but relaxing. Not the best for sure, like sometimes, I get shitty customers. Y'know, the kind who forget that people who serve them are people too. If they keep bothering me, I ask them to step aside so I can assist the next customer. Even if there isn't another customer.

I'm kind of getting to understand why you work in that bar all the time. Something rewarding about routine labor. Helps that I'm getting compensated decently though. I'd definitely be slacking off more if I wasn't. Not that I'm not already slacking.

It's beautiful here. I know that's what everybody says when they travel and "it's beautiful" doesn't mean anything to you; doesn't communicate the beauty since I can't think of the exact words, and even then, they're just words. You're not here to see what I see. I haven't even taken any photos really. But I need to say it anyway.

There's this dock with a lighthouse at the end that I like to go out to. It's kind of a spot for teens here. Oh, you'd like this. One time I went out with a bottle of red wine (don't remember the kind—probably some regular table stuff—I'm not a fucking gourmet like you), because this was before I found a trustworthy weed dealer, you know, and sat and drank and listened to the waves and looked out onto the horizon. Then this pair of teenagers, probably like sixteen, one boy and one girl, came around and joined me. They were super friendly. We tried to talk, met somewhere between their rudimentary English and my near-nonexistent French, and I managed to find out that they had been best friends since they were five and that they were both looking to study abroad next year, though they weren't sure where.

For the most part though, we just sat together and passed the bottle around, appreciated the sound of waves lapping against the dock.

I guess I ought to explain myself. Try to.

Question: Why am I writing to you?

Answer: I dunno. I didn't plan to do it. After writing to Joshua, I just got this impulse to write to you. I mean, writing to Joshua is obvious. Of course I'm going to write to him. I'm going to write six encyclopedias to him. You, on the other hand... I guess that answer is complicated.

We don't have that much history. But what little history we do have feels profound in one way or another. I'm sure you feel that way about it too. To put it bluntly, it's definitely not as intense on my side. I don't think about you every day. I'm not motivated to impress you.

But still... I don't know. I think about you sometimes.

Let me dissect you as I would a character in a boring novel for AP English. This character takes a passive role despite seeing himself as the protagonist of his story. He is willing to allow people to bitch at him relentlessly, to absorb all their bullshit. He observes, perhaps quietly judging, with this distant look in his eye. I feel resentful toward this character sometimes. An instinctive reaction to this attitude. Still, he's a profoundly ordinary character. Frustratingly polite. A character can absolutely be too polite, by the way. I think he thinks he's subtly suggesting his perspectives when he's really letting them go ignored. But still, this attitude makes him sort of interesting. Maybe because he listens. Actually listens. There's something emasculating about it, which I'll admit is a turn off, but there's also something sorta... supreme about it. Enlightened? This is a character who makes the people around him reflect on themselves, whether he knows it or not. He does this with this self-effacing grace, this inability to insist upon himself as an active agent, his presence in the present moment. I feel above and below him. He's boring and engrossing and everything in between.

There's this girl I know who's a few years older than us. Junior in college. She'd been dating this guy for a year and a half, right? They both went to community college, but once she graduated, she transferred to a bigger university to get her bachelor's. The guy stayed behind because he couldn't afford it yet. She told me that this was the boy she was probably going to end up marrying. But after a semester she broke up with him, said the distance was taking too much of a toll.

Their friends thought it would just be a temporary thing, that they'd make up when she came home for the summer. Instead, she started dating this other guy and they've been together for a long time now.

Have you ever understood both sides of a conflict too well and realized there's no way you can side with either? And if either saw the conflict from the other person's side, things could be resolved more gracefully? But they can't because that's impossible, and so they live the rest of their lives resentful of one another, splitting up their friends and family in the process, isolating everyone from each other more and more than before?

I'm not a good writer and don't really know how to make this flow well, so this is taking me a long time. It's hard to figure out the things I want to tell you. Or how to tell them to you. I'll keep writing though. Maybe arrive at a thesis.

I cried a few times when I first got here. I think I expected too much. Somebody told me that the maladies of the soul can't be cured by moving the body. Maybe I heard it in a song. I don't remember. It's not untrue, though I can't see how a change of scenery wouldn't help. I'd have gone insane if I had to stay at home. I'm completely confident in that. Like, obviously a small French seaside town with centuries of history and culture will beat out a boring antiseptic Midwestern suburb.

God, I'm so lucky. I have all these opportunities. I was able to just casually fuck off to France, and meanwhile, so many people are wallowing in the same bullshit places they always have and probably always will.

Someone I met offered me a job with this anti-discrimination nonprofit helping Muslim people in France. It pays less than the gelato cart and requires probably four times the work. I'm thinking about taking it, though. Although the white savior-ism of a white girl from the Midwest traveling to a foreign country to battle oppression while she's on a journey of self-discovery makes me sick, I can't scoop gelato forever. And maybe it'll help me feel better to help other people for a change, despite the optics of it.

I feel like I know even less about myself than before. More questions, no answers.

But it's peaceful for now. And I'm never bored.

We never did talk about our parents. I wish I'd asked more about your mom. You got so dark whenever I brought it up. You don't owe me anything so it's not like I'm demanding to know. It was just out-of-character. You showed me an emotion for once. Kind of a turn-on, actually. I bet you think it's bad to express negative emotions like that. I'd rather you not walk on eggshells. Better to just stomp them down and deal with the aftermath later. It's more fun that way. More exciting.

There's a sort of connection among kids raised by single parents, don't you think?

I might as well tell you what happened. It's not as if it's a suppressed memory or something. Not running from my past or whatever. I just don't like talking about it because I've gone over it too many times. You ever have certain topics you've obsessed about for so long you get sick of them? And you don't want to talk about them ever again for no reason beyond how you've gone over them so many times, you've accepted there's nothing more to be done? This is one of those deals.

It could be summed up in a paragraph, a sentence. Two words. He cheated.

Our dad was a high school teacher. Social studies, world history. Summary: Hot student teacher shows up during a time period in which my workaholic mom remained mostly at the hospital and ignored the emotional and sexual needs of our dad.

I've never asked my mom exactly how she found out. It took a long time for her to even tell us about the affair. Imagine that: Your dad just disappears without a reason one day, and it never clicks until years later.

The guilt must have destroyed him. He sends money that we don't need and that I doubt he can afford to give up. Like, imagine a high school teacher thinking he needs to support a surgeon. He seems to think it fills in for his absence. And like we've had nannies, babysitters. Real good ones. But they just take care of us. It would be different if he hadn't been there at the beginning. It would be different if we didn't know that he could come back at any time but chooses not to.

I try to see him, but he won't budge. He lives really far away now. Doesn't respond to my letters, my calls or emails. Hasn't quite forgiven himself, I guess. In English class once, we talked about when Nabokov, who lived the most structured and unexciting adulthood imaginable, had one affair and nearly killed himself over it. I guess it's something like that. Just an absurd amount of self-laceration. My mom's basically over the whole thing now, oddly enough. She wants for them to be friends again. But he's stubborn, impossibly stubborn. Stubborn to the point where he doesn't realize his absence is worse than the reason he left in the first place.

Or, I don't know. I haven't seen him in years. Things could have changed. It's possible that he's built a new life and doesn't want to go back to the old one anymore.

I miss him, yeah. Hardly remember him though. I hope I get to see him before the memory gets too vague. God, I hope I recognize him next time I see him. If I ever do.

Side note, I promise I will beat the shit out of you if you ever say I have daddy issues. I don't think you would, but just a fair warning. I've done it before.

The divorce and subsequent absent father definitely cast a shadow over our childhood. Joshua got really dark. I hid it as much as possible. You and I have one specific thing in common: We're good at looking like we fit in, when we're really critical of everything. Joshua was never able to get into that swing. He's good at being alone. He worries me, actually. He's stronger in some ways and weaker in others. You two might get along well. He likes weird sci-fi movies and anime and shit. Documentaries about mushrooms. Could never get into that stuff myself. It bores the crap out of me.

You should introduce him to the world of fashion, too. Take him shopping. I'm tired of the black hoodies.

Friends. Sometimes, my friends feel more like subordinates. Is that egotistical to say? But it's true. They're clearly my sycophants. It's so weird being looked up to like that. No, not even looked up to. Mimicked. Like I've got all these shadows. It's terrible, actually. I mean, having all these people around you who idolize you instead of trying to understand you. Like, when they hang out with me, they see me how they want to see me, not as a real fluid person. Is this just a natural ability to get people to flock around me? Am I predestined fan bait? Do I have some kind of pheromone? Or just mega-extroverted or something…

Self-reflection is hard. I keep doubting everything I write down. Maybe that's why I hang out with those types. They don't challenge me at all. They don't expect me to change, be better.

That said, I hate how everyone characterizes me as the "not like the other girls" girl. Even if my friends have problems being their own independent people, there's a reason why I'm drawn to them. I like the same shit they like. I'm not much different from them.

Writing to you instead of one of them feels like I'm feeding into the patriarchy or something. Pissing off the third wave. (Wait, which wave are we on now?) Look at me in this letter, quivering at your heels, my words making me more and more vulnerable by the minute.

You never had delusions of "saving me," I'll give you that. I've had enough assholes try to play that card. In fact you're aside from all that, aren't you? That's how it feels when we hang out. You're not looking to subscribe to some vision of masculinity in your head. You're not one of those scumbags who thinks they're so sensitive because they write poems and read Haruki Murakami and own Criterion Blu-rays. No, when we hang out, it feels like we're in this bubble—this tiny isolated plain of existence. No shallow gossip, no bullshit comments about the weather or whatever. No treating me differently because I'm a girl. You totally want me, that's obvious, but I also don't really feel you pushing me into anything.

I'm only reminded of how I'm alive when I do something new. I have an aversion to repetitive lifestyles. Like, all my nicest memories seem to involve strangers. Like just recently at this train station. I met this super sweet German couple who were wandering around the country. We were the only people in the area and we were waiting like an hour for the train. They told me all about themselves, where they'd been. They felt like an old couple, even though they were probably in their late twenties. Something real "old soul" about them. Really made traveling in the countryside at night less nerve wracking.

It's unlikely I'll ever see them again. Isn't that wonderful though? One perfect concise intersection of lives. That doesn't happen back home. Everyone and everything is too familiar. I guess that's what happens when you stay still for too long. It's not bad, not exactly. I just didn't realize how much I felt like a zombie most of the time, until I broke out of the habit. Kind of scares me.

Life here is getting kind of repetitive, tell you the truth. It's still fresh enough so that it doesn't bother me, but I do wonder when the zombie feeling will hit. And it brings up other issues. Like, what if I'm never able to settle down? Why do I even feel so much pressure to eventually settle down?

My idea of a good life is to keep moving, let myself slowly erode away in the wind, till I'm a pile of dust. I'll stop and appreciate the intersections with other lives for sure. You just can't expect me to double back and stay at one.

It gets lonely here, I'll admit. But I'd rather be lonely than sick of being around the people I care about. Do you get me? You must get me. If you don't, you're probably going to obsess over it until you do. Probably going to use words like "ruminate."

Yeah, don't pretend like I don't know you.

Local boys are generally idiots here too. You just can't wear pants that tight and expect me to believe your penis is as big as you say it is. There's something weirdly comforting about how stupidity is universal. They just smoke and talk and make fun of tourists, people they find below them. They've talked shit at me for my poor grasp of French while simultaneously requesting in broken English that I blow them behind the lighthouse. At least they aren't aggressive, I suppose. Not like that's much of a silver lining. "I have to put up with way-too-forward requests for sex every day, but that's okay because at least I'm not brute forced into it!" The bar is on the floor.

I may leave soon. That job I was offered wouldn't start for a few months anyway. Maybe I'll go to Spain? It's right there, after all. I love how close everything is here. Drive an hour or so and you're in another country. Back home, if you drive for an hour, you'll just hit another strip mall. And so much tradition, history. We killed off all our history, didn't we? Even post-colonial history has been paved over. There's no real culture back home, no background to have any connection to. It's just football and parking lot drug dealers. Not that people are much better here, but it feels so much emptier back home.

Maybe it's just the familiarity though.

It's true, okay. I did feed off of your attention. I liked that you have "feelings" for me. That you "like" me. I wish you wouldn't. It's not like I wouldn't enjoy it to some degree, but I guess I've always found something evil and possessive about monogamous relationships in general. Nothing against you personally. I don't want anybody to expect me to always be at their side, because I'm not. There are just things I don't want anybody's help with. I need people. I know I can't be on my own entirely, but I don't need to be in whatever a serious long-term paired-off romantic relationship is either.

But then, hell, I'm only eighteen. I've never been "in love." At this point, a relationship just sounds ridiculous to me. Definition: A unique partnership in which both parties connect on an emotional, intellectual, and perhaps even spiritual level, while occasionally grabbing each other's genitals and putting their tongues in each other's mouths.

I mean, if you can look at all the negatives and still go for it, then more power to you.

I can't find anything too wrong with people who go for casual relationships… I mean, we all have urges. We all need release. But there's something wrong with it. Sex without love, that is. For me at least. Thinking about it makes me feel so empty.

It's just really complicated. Maybe I'm afraid of complicated things.

Okay. The alcohol must be addressed. You, my dear boy, romanticize self-destructive behavior. Put the Bukowski away. I bet you sit there some nights with a bottle of wine and think about how deep you are. No, really, it bothers me. I like a drink once in a while, but you go beyond. I thought I was being childish at first, thinking things like "Well, why can't you be happy sober?" or "Why do you have to be drunk to have fun?" They're legitimate questions though. Maybe I've never asked because I don't feel like I have any authority.

Let me observe instead, eh? You drink. You drink often. You enjoy this image people have of you as this well-dressed, well-bred, reserved white boy from a long line of well-dressed, well-bred, reserved white boys. You may conceal it with sophisticated methods of preparation and needlepoint attention to taste, but the fact remains that you drink to get drunk. And that is the crucial factor. You like how it changes you. You explained it to me. You enjoy the way it "makes people more honest." You use booze as a device to make people open up to you. You aren't a frat boy who sexually assaults girls at parties, no. Instead you drain information from everyone. Suck up all our words and categorize them somewhere in your head. Gather secrets. Judge.

You don't need to know everything about everyone. I believe that. You can't anyway. That's the difference between us. You can't handle living in the fog. I can't imagine life without it.

Would it hurt you to know the amount of guys I slept with when we were doing... whatever we were doing? I'm not sure. I feel a satisfaction in the attempt though. Like, there's something about you that feels worth hurting. Like it's necessary. But unfortunately, I didn't sleep with that many guys since I met you. Only a couple. You probably know them, in passing at least. And now you might spend the rest of your days wondering which guys they were. Muahaha.

I meant it when I said I expected more of you. It's not just the privilege. I mean, that's definitely a part of it. But it's that extremely unusual mixture of privilege and sympathy. Of being unassuming and sensitive when you could, in fact, be a loud piece of shit and receive absolutely no blow-back for it. I'm in kind of a similar situation in that my mom will probably cover my college, if I ever get to that, and I will probably always have her as a safety net, if I'm ever in a bad place. But I'm weak and stubborn and whenever anyone tells me about their problems, I either dictatorially tell them what to do or fuck off with some distraction, because I can't be bothered with the stress of other people's problems. Is that an unfair judgment of myself? I mean, even Dennis... I wanted to help him. But I mostly felt guilty on my brother's behalf for something. Maybe, if you get to know him, he'll tell you about that. The point is, I helped him because I felt obligated to. And I don't know how to live with that.

I want to see you on book sleeves one day. I want to see you on stage, speaking with that calm voice of yours, teaching people how to be better than they are. Manifesting a gentler, softer world through how you observe it. I want that so bad.

And for me... I don't know yet. I'm so fucking lucky, man. I feel like I could stay here forever if I wanted. Not that I want to but... I feel like I have the power to convince the people in charge of this program to let me stay forever. I could learn French and get knocked up and live in the countryside alone with all my children running around the house, baking pies and tending my garden. Or that doesn't sound like me much, does it? Still, it's a nice thought.

You can't go back home. I read that somewhere. You can't go back home. I'm gone, never to return. Now I have to look for somewhere else to be. Find my sanctum.

I'll come back to the states one day. I'm pretty sure of that. The guilt of leaving Joshua is too much sometimes. Maybe find another strange little suburb to dwell in. Somewhere familiar but different. Invite Joshua to join, if ever, whenever, he wants.

I want to be someone who at least one person can depend on.

I still listen to Bill Evans sometimes. I don't want you to think I like you, but it would be rude of me not to tell you that.

You and I will never know why Dennis killed himself. I mean, I have a good idea of the reasons, the facts leading him to the emotions, to the rash action... but I don't know what he went through in his head to get to the point where he actually did it.

We can't know his thoughts. We won't.

That hurt me a lot at first. I wanted to get rid of all the fog surrounding him. God, that's why I let you get him so drunk. He wouldn't open up. I thought just a little bit...

No, no use blaming you or me. No use with blame, full stop. What could we have done? Tell me that. Short of monitoring the kid every day all day, short of drilling into his brain and installing an impulse control device, what could we have done? Short of Joshua... God, I so badly want you to know something that is not my place to tell. If only. Let me say that. If only. But all of it is impossible, all of it comes with its own set of baggage. Maybe it was inevitable, and if things were different, it would only have delayed Dennis killing himself by a year or two. Maybe the universe in which Dennis doesn't die is far too statistically improbable.

It doesn't matter, though. No matter how much I wonder what could have been. How much I doubt what I did. I'm sure we established that we cared about him. Established that we would be sad if anything were to happen to him. That's about all we can do. His mind was made up. He was sick of the fog, way sicker than you could ever be, and he wanted out.

Or, fuck, maybe he wasn't sure. I mean, obviously, he wasn't sure. Nobody is every sure about that sort of thing. Self-annihilation isn't a decision, it's an action. He didn't decide it, he did it.

We have to live with the consequences of his action.

He had to die with them.

I'm alive, okay? And I'm going to keep living. Dennis will haunt me from time to time. But then, so will you. So will everything I'm leaving behind. That's fine. The question will keep coming to me: Why do I keep living? Why the hell do I keep living? And I've got to keep trying to answer that.

Those two French kids I told you about earlier? They told me something I've been thinking about ever since. See, I asked them if they knew a dealer. And, lo and behold, they did. Next time I met up with them, after conducting business with a fine entrepreneur in the shadows behind a bakery, we passed a joint between the three of us at the lighthouse.

"It helps with the blues," the boy told me.

"What?" I said.

"Louis Armstrong," he said, eyeing the joint. "He say, it helps with the blues."

I laughed like crazy at that. I love it. What better way to sum up every way we try to cope with the collective pile of every bullshit thing big and small that bothers us, depresses us. We're just trying to find something that helps.

Fuck, man. I can't stop thinking about you, the way you looked at me. Always with expectation. Always... wanting. What do you really want from me? Why am I so fascinating?

No, really. I'm curious.

What do you want?

Afterword

It Helps with the Blues was written by and then for my teenage self.

It began as a short story titled "Jukebox Waltz" that I wrote for a creative writing class when I was 16. It was inspired by the song "Waltz #2" by Elliott Smith. The story shares a similar foundation as the novel you've just read, but I wasn't satisfied with the outcome. Like most teenage writing experiments, it felt rushed, sentimental, and confused. But I liked the premise of a boy observing the world around him a la Nick Carraway, and I knew the near-rural suburban Midwestern setting was something that I would never see depicted unless someone like me did it. So I kept working on it, later revising the story into a novella.

The first two chapters came to me easily—even early drafts aren't so different from the final product in this book today. But the rest was an uphill battle. I must have rewritten the third chapter a dozen times, and I wrote the rest on and off throughout college. Eventually I finished it. I showed it to some friends and halfheartedly queried it to agents, but like most halfhearted actions this went nowhere. I liked the story and thought it was good enough at best, but was too tired of tinkering with a 20,000 word novella when I could have been working on something else. I didn't know what to do with it, so I shelved it for years.

Then, in 2019, I decided to expand the novella into a short novel. I reread it and found a number of areas in need of expansion, most notably the roles of Joshua and

Estelle. And now that I had some distance from young adult emotions, I could approach them more reflectively than I did before. The wounds weren't as fresh and I could observe them from all angles. There's a line in the François Truffaut movie *Bed and Board* when the main character's wife is talking to him about how he's writing a novel based on his difficult childhood: "If you use art to settle accounts, it's no longer art." For me, writing as an adult years away from what triggered me to write the novel in the first place meant no longer writing to settle accounts. The process eased.

Blues then developed into something I knew I could be proud to call my debut, something full of queer intimacy, volatile emotions, and inimitable Midwestern beauty that—and this is just a fact, not boasting—only I could have made.

It's funny to think of a short novel—less than 50,000 words—as having a decade-long gestation period, but hey, it all went somewhere. I'm a very different person than I was when I was 16, I'm even a very different person than I was in 2019, but I still believe in what I made here, and I'm extremely pleased to finally send this work out into the world. These characters are very near and dear to my heart—made up as they are of parts of me and parts of the people who grew up around me. It's wonderful to finally be able to let them go.

Acknowledgments

Thank you to J. Scott Coatsworth from Other Worlds Ink, who accepted my short story "From the Sun and Scorched Earth" into the *Fix the World* anthology. This was my first fiction publication.

Thank you to Adam Kranz, Kevin Craig, Tucker Lieberman, and Anton Prosser for providing invaluable guidance in proofreading the manuscript.

Thank you to Ryszard I. Merey for the opportunity to publish this novel with tRaum Books and for your under-the-microscope editorial oversight, which helped make this book so much stronger than I ever could have made it on my own.

Thank you to Oliver Grin for your gorgeous cover art, not to mention all your love and support over the years.

And, of course, thank you to my parents, Tom and Kathy, and my brothers, Kevin and Dan, for all their love and support from day one.

Full gratitude as well to all the friends and acquaintances who I grew up with in our small town in northern Illinois. All of you helped shape this novel. Even the ones I never liked.

About the author

Bryan Cebulski is a writer from Illinois living in the woods of Northern California who specializes in a quiet strain of queer fiction. He is a jack-of-all-trades working as a reporter. *It Helps with the Blues* is his first novel.

tRaum books

Is a tiny press dedicated to unconventional formats, with a focus on queer and trans narratives. You can visit us online at

http://www.traumbooks.com

A warm thank you

To the following people, for making this book possible:

Dermitzel
Brak
Jun Nozaki
Leon Sorensen
Clacks
Agnes Merey
Gele Croom
Philip O'Loughlin
Steven Askew
Tucker Lieberman
Lachelle Seville

Your support is seen, felt, and appreciated so much. Because of you, we can continue to put out the books we believe in.

If you'd like to support our press as well, you can find us over at

https://www.patreon.com/tRaumbooks.